M000165317

NO GUTS, NO FURY

FEDERAL BUREAU OF MAGIC COZY MYSTERY, BOOK 3

ANNABEL CHASE

RED PALM PRESS LLC

CHAPTER ONE

"SHOW ME YOUR WINGS," my father said.

"Excuse me?" My fork hovered midway between my plate and my mouth.

"Stanley, she's eating," Sally scolded him. "You don't demand to see your daughter's wings during breakfast. It's rude."

"What's rude is to show them to her mother, but not her father," he said. "Who taught you to ride a bike? Or to get revenge on your worst enemy without them realizing it was you?"

I frowned. "You realize those two aren't remotely equivalent things, right?"

"They are to me," my father said firmly.

There was no reasoning with a vengeance demon, not when he felt insulted. "I didn't want to show the wings to Mom either." As a fury, all my powers weren't granted at birth, so a new set of wings was a big deal. The more I used my powers, the more traits I'd acquire over time. My biggest fear was that my rare and impressive powers would corrupt me and I'd eventually succumb to the dark side.

1

"Then why did you? Just admit you like her better." My father leaned back in his chair like a petulant child.

"To be honest, neither of you ranks very high at the moment." This morning, my mother told me I looked like Johnny Depp after a week at sea. "But I made a deal"—with the devil that was Beatrice Fury, black magic witch extraordinaire—"that was the only reason I agreed."

My father slurped down his orange juice. "Fine, then I'll make a deal with you, too. Show me your wings and I promise not to take the job over on Gorgonzola Way."

I set down my fork and stared at him. "What job?"

My father shrugged. "A small act of revenge, that's all."

"That's *all*?" I repeated. "You're not supposed to be taking jobs in this territory. You swore."

"You did swear, Stanley," Sally said. She dislodged a piece of bacon from her fang. "It isn't fair to renege on a promise."

I was pleased that my stepmom seemed to have my back. It was hard enough to live in Chipping Cheddar after years of trying to stay away. I didn't need my dad to flaunt his demonic misdeeds in the face of authority—my face, specifically.

"So what?" my father said, visibly annoyed. "Since when does a vengeance demon keep his word?"

Sally smacked his arm. "It's one thing to break a vow to a client, but family is another matter."

My father was undeterred. "I'm your father and I've asked to see your wings. Don't disrespect me, Eden."

"They're *my* wings," I huffed. The enormous black feathers had sprouted from my back after an unexpected brush with a vampire during an FBI assignment triggered my siphoning power. I inadvertently sucked the vampire's power and then sucked my FBI partner's blood. Not a good career move. The FBI transferred me from San Francisco to the Federal Bureau of Magic outpost in my hometown.

"Knock if off, Stanley. It's Eden's body. If she doesn't want to show you, then you need to respect her wishes."

"My body, my rules," I said.

"Well, those wings aren't going to do anything to improve that poor posture of yours," my father said.

"I didn't exactly ask for them," I said. If it were up to me, I'd have no fury powers at all. Normal humans dreamed of having superpowers and I dreamed of being a normal human. The grass was always greener...

"You should strengthen your core muscles," my father said. "That'll help with your posture issues."

"Your father's been doing one-armed pushups," Sally said.

My father pointed his fork at me. "You should try those."

"I'll be sure to start right after breakfast," I said.

"Don't get fresh with me, young lady," my father said.

Why I thought breakfast at my father's house would be better than my mother's, I had no idea. Each house came with its own baggage.

"Ease up, Stanley," Sally said. "You complain that she doesn't visit enough and, now that she's here, all you're doing is giving her a hard time."

He wiped his chin with his napkin. "She's only five hundred yards away. It's not a hardship to see us."

My parents divorced when I was ten. As part of the divorce agreement, they divided the marital property and my father built a house on his half, so it was easy to bounce between the two. Although they lived separate lives, they were united in their desire to torture me.

"And that's why I'm here now," I said, "but I do need to get to the office."

"See?" Sally said. "Eden's an adult with her own busy life."

"Not so much busy as annoying," I said. "There's an FBM training agent arriving today. They want me to complete a two-week course since my formal training was with the FBI."

3

"What's there to learn?" my father asked. "You get a whiff that something supernatural's out of whack and you pounce." He slammed his fist on the table.

"If it were as simple as that, I'd be pouncing all over Munster Close," I replied. "This whole cul-de-sac is out of whack."

"Not Mrs. Paulson," Sally said.

My father snorted. "She's out of whack for different reasons."

As one of the few humans living on our street, the elderly neighbor stood out among the vampires, demons, and other supernaturals here, not that Mrs. Paulson had any clue. Only humans with the Sight could see that we were different. To Mrs. Paulson, we were simply weird and loud.

"She's harmless," I said. Nosy to a fault, but harmless.

My father gaped at me. "Harmless? She called Mick a few years back because she'd seen your mother and grandmother burning someone in effigy in the backyard. Turns out the old bat had cut a hole in the fence to spy on them. Your mother had to conjure a scarecrow before Mick made it to the back-yard and pretend it had accidentally caught fire."

Mick O'Neill had been the chief of police in Chipping Cheddar for many years until his recent death at the hands of a fear demon. My father and the chief had been friends, though not so close that he knew about my family's super-natural origins. As a fury, I was able to communicate with his ghost after his death and helped to solve his murder, but I hadn't seen him since then. I assumed he was able to move on.

"I have no doubt Grandma took care of the hole in the fence," I said.

"Took care of more than that," my father replied. "Mrs. Paulson went temporarily blind for a week. I only know because I saw her daughter driving her everywhere."

That didn't surprise me. Grandma was quicker to hex than forgive.

"You should take some food to the office," Sally said. "It can't hurt to offer your visitor a homemade muffin."

"Good thinking," I said. I swiped a couple of blueberry muffins from the plate on the table. "I'm not above bribery."

My father cast a sidelong glance at me. "Well, I guess I finally know where the ethical line is with you."

"Yes, bribery with baked goods," I said. "Make a note of it."

I took the scenic route on my way to the office, passing rows of pretty historical buildings that become more prevalent the closer you get to the Chesapeake Bay. Chipping Cheddar, Maryland was settled by English Puritans with surnames like Abbot, Bradford, and Danforth. Some founders turned to the water for their livelihood, while others chose dairy farming and eventually cheesemaking, as evidenced by the names of the town streets.

In the distance, I glimpsed the promenade that runs along the waterfront—a popular option for walkers, joggers, and cyclists.

I parked on seedy Asiago Street and made sure to lock the car doors. While an office with a water view would've been nice, ours is flanked by a donut shop and a tattoo parlor. Unsurprisingly, I try to spend as much time out of the office as possible.

My hands were full of muffins, so I pushed open the door with my bottom and entered backwards. "Neville, you should probably put up the ward before Trainy McTrain-erson gets here. Better yet, glamour the door to look like a brick wall so he can't find it." I laughed. "That would be…"

I turned and stopped short in front of a tall, slender man with an angular face. His golden hair was cut short and his ears were slightly pointed at the tips. He wore a black suit with a plain white shirt and a burgundy tie. Think *Lord of the Rings* meets *Men In Black*.

His bright blue eyes fixed on me. "Trainy McTrainerson reporting for duty. Agent Fury, I presume?"

"Yes," I squeaked.

"Most benevolent one," Neville interrupted. "May I present Agent Quinn Redmond?"

I peered around Agent Redmond to glare at my assistant. "You could have presented him a little sooner," I said.

Agent Redmond nodded in Neville's direction. "Not to worry. Mr. Wyman has been accommodating."

I scrutinized him. "You're fae."

"Very good, Agent Fury. I suppose we can cross 'identification of species' off our training list and move on to more advanced work."

The sarcasm was strong in this one. "It's just that I expected a wizard or a warlock."

"You think fae aren't as capable?"

Now seemed like a good time to make an offering. I thrust out a hand. "Muffin?"

He stared at the baked good as though I'd offered him a deep fried tarantula. "No, thank you. I'm not one for carbs."

"Your loss." I extended the muffin toward Neville. "Come on. You know you want one."

Neville licked his lips. "I do like a good muffin." He reached forward, but then halted. "You didn't make them, did you?"

I snorted. "I like you too much to inflict my baking skills upon you, Neville."

"I have your latte," Neville said.

"A fair trade then." He took the muffin and handed me a cup with The Daily Grind logo.

"Thanks, you're the best." I spun around and went to my

6

desk, where I switched on the sun lamp and dropped into my chair. "I wasn't expecting you this early, Agent Redmond."

"Clearly." He hovered between the desks. "Should we begin?"

"Can I at least have a minute to get settled? I'm not much good before my first latte."

Agent Redmond's mouth formed a thin line. "I'll be sure to alert the criminals not to trouble you until after nine."

I held up a finger. "Weekdays only. I sleep in on the weekends."

"Not while I'm in town, I'm afraid," Agent Redmond said. "The next two weeks will be intensive because we have a lot of ground to cover."

I grumbled under my breath.

"Will I be needed during the training sessions, Agent Redmond?" Neville asked.

"I'll let you know which ones," he replied. "We'll include a few team building exercises."

Neville clapped his hands together. "Oh, excellent."

My expression remained deadpan. "Yes. Goody."

"Now Agent Fury, you must understand that training is necessary," Agent Redmond said. "Most FBM agents were trained at our headquarters, much like your Quantico."

I folded my arms. "Then maybe you should have sent one of those agents to take over for Paul Pidcock instead of me." I'd basically been strong-armed into taking the position once I was considered too dangerous for the FBI.

"To be frank, that would've been my preference," Agent Redmond said, "but I'm not in charge of such matters."

As I drank my latte, my body began to relax. "What's first on the training agenda then?"

"Paperwork," Agent Redmond replied. "We'll go through the rules and regulations."

"I did provide her with that information," Neville interjected, not wanting to be seen as a slacker.

Agent Redmond glanced at Neville over his broad shoulder. "I'm sure you did, but it's helpful to review it together. There will be a written test at the end of the training period, as well as a simulation exercise."

"I was told there would be no math," I said.

Neville brought over the official binder and set it on my desk.

"Thank you, Mr. Wyman," Agent Redmond said. "We'll start with the basics and go from there."

I suddenly wished I'd lingered at my father's, even shown him my wings. Regrets.

Agent Redmond leaned over my shoulder and pointed to the first paragraph. "Secrecy is paramount. You must not reveal your true nature or the existence of this agency to any human."

"Unless they have the Sight," I said. "My best friend Clara is an empath with the Sight, so she knows all about us."

"If you continue to subparagraph 1(a)(3), you'll see that empaths are one of the exceptions, as are psychics."

"I don't need rules to tell me not to blab about our existence. It's not like I want to advertise the fact that I'm a fury."

"She's self-loathing," Neville offered from across the room.

I resisted the urge to stick out my tongue. There was likely a maturity rule buried somewhere in the binder.

"I don't understand that attitude," Agent Redmond said stiffly, and continued to plow through the first section of the binder.

"Of course not," I said. "You're fae. You probably spent your youth frolicking through meadows and communing with butterflies."

He cleared his throat. "Do I seem the type to frolic, Agent Fury?"

I hastened a glance at his somber expression. "Maybe not now, dressed in your expensive straight jacket, but dollars to donuts you weren't always like this."

The agent flinched. "Like what?"

"Agent Fury, might I suggest not insulting the training instructor?" Neville said.

"It wasn't meant as an insult," I said, somewhat apologetic. I would have preferred a childhood of unicorns and rainbows over blood and brimstone. Unfortunately, my childhood wasn't a 'choose your own adventure' story. It was more of a duck and cover story, with each family member a potential nuclear bomb of evil.

"Let's get back to the rules, shall we?" Agent Redmond said. "Then we can move on to more interesting matters."

"Sure." I picked up a muffin and bit into it, spraying crumbs all over the page.

Agent Redmond flicked the debris away with an elegant finger. "Perhaps we should add 'no food or drink during training' to the rules?"

I flashed a plastic smile. "Only if you want to see me go full fury."

"How about we save that for the simulation exercise?" he replied.

I set the muffin aside and returned my attention to the text. Did I really have to endure two weeks of Agent Uptight and Serious?

The longer I lived, the more convinced I was that the universe hated me.

CHAPTER TWO

I WOKE up the next morning in a foul mood. I'd spent hours with Agent Redmond yesterday, going through the rules and regulations in excruciating detail. Even Neville had dozed off at one point, prompting Agent Redmond to give a shrill whistle to put an end to the snoring. I had a feeling today wouldn't be much better. Part of me hoped a winged monkey demon would swoop down and steal a puppy so that I had something more important to do.

Reluctantly, I swung my legs over the side of the mattress and stretched.

"Good morning, Eden." Alice Wentworth's ethereal body drifted out of a dusty box. The Wentworths were one of Chipping Cheddar's founding families and this had once been their farmhouse.

"Is it, though?" I asked.

Alice moved to the window at the back of the attic. "John's progress on the barn is slow. I've been watching him work." The barn from the old dairy farm was in the process of being renovated as my new home. In the mean-time, I slept on a mattress in the attic of my mother's house and tried to steer clear of family drama. Easier said than done.

"I know," I said, "but it's okay. He does great work and it's nice to know he's enjoying it." John Maclaren had recently been the victim of a scales demon. Thanks to the demon's interference, John had won the lottery, bought a boat, and planned to abandon carpentry to write the Great American Novel. When good luck turned bad, however, John realized that he truly loved his work and wanted to continue his trade regardless of his bank account. A rich man in every way. Truth be told, I envied him.

"You're not concerned with staying here too long?" Alice asked, gesturing to the attic.

"I was here too long the moment I walked through the door from San Francisco," I said. "I'll manage, though."

I dressed quickly and ran a brush through my dark hair. I'd convinced Agent Redmond to meet me at The Daily Grind. By convinced, I mean that I lied and told him I had a morning dentist appointment that was conveniently located right by the best coffee shop in town.

"Before you go, will you help me with the television?" Alice asked.

"Oh, of course, I almost forgot." An older model television was now nestled on top of one of the storage boxes. I'd asked my brother to set it up so that Alice could watch what she wanted, instead of being subjected to whatever my family had on downstairs.

"It can wait if you're in a rush," Alice said. "I don't mind the game shows. Some of them can be quite challenging."

I hunted for the remote. "Up here you can use one of my subscriptions to watch movies or TV shows," I said. "Goddess knows there are more options than time." I hesitated. "Well, maybe not for you."

Alice glanced nervously at the television. "How will I

know where to start? I don't want to stumble on anything inappropriate."

I found the remote under the mattress. "Alice, you've been dead for well over a century. Everything you see will be inappropriate." I clicked on the power button. "Here, I'll set up your profile and then the recommendation engine will make suggestions based on your preferences."

Alice drifted closer to watch the screen. "Ooh, I like this idea."

I created a profile called 'Alice' and chose a ghost avatar for her.

"Can't I be that cute little kitten head instead?" Alice asked. "I'm already a ghost."

I changed her avatar to the kitten. "All you need to do is click the buttons on the remote to find what you want. They're all labeled." Alice's interactions with the physical world were minimal, but I knew she was capable of that much.

"How exciting," she said. "It's like opening the portal to a new world. Thank you, Eden."

I groaned. "Do me a favor. Don't mention portals and new worlds." The whole reason there was an FBM outpost in Chipping Cheddar was due to the dormant portal to Otherworld, the supernatural realm, located in the hillside adjacent to Davenport Park, known locally as 'the mound.' Thanks to the portal's mystical energy, the town is a magnet for supernaturals in the human world.

Once Alice was happily scrolling for shows, I crept downstairs for breakfast, hoping the coast was clear. I wasn't in the mood to deal with my family, not that I ever was.

"You're leaving the house like that?" My mother's critical voice stopped me in my tracks.

Nope. The coast was definitely not clear.

"I'm not leaving the house," I replied, turning to face her. "I'm having breakfast first."

My mother continued to scrutinize me. "Well, you'd better leave yourself plenty of time to go back upstairs and change."

I glanced down at my plain blue T-shirt and capris. "What's wrong with this?"

"What isn't wrong with it?" my mother replied. "You'll never catch anyone's eye in an outfit like that. You look like you stepped out of a Sears catalogue."

"Is that even a thing anymore?" I asked.

My mother gave me a knowing look. "Exactly."

I brushed past her and went to the island to grab an apple from the fruit bowl. My grandmother hovered near the stovetop, waiting for Aunt Thora to pour the tea.

"Don't mind her. Your mother's on everyone's nerves today," Grandma said. "I'm still waiting for an apology."

My mother groaned. "Again with this?"

"Again?" Grandma shot back. "You're the one who started it."

My mother threw up her hands in exasperation. "I don't even know what I did, let alone how I started it."

Grandma wagged a finger at her. "You know what you did."

"I don't, Mom. It was your dream." My mother went to the table and handed Ryan a cheese stick. My one-year-old nephew seemed pleased with this offering and shoved it into his mouth, his cheeks puffing as he chewed.

Grandma's eyes flashed with annoyance. "You know as well as I do that dreams are messages, which means you did something. Stop denying it."

"Sometimes dreams are just dreams," my mother snapped.

She kept her back to Grandma, avoiding her steely gaze. I didn't blame her. I tended to hide when either one of them

13

waved a finger or stared at me a beat too long. You never knew when black magic would come flying out at you. They both had a tendency to act impetuously, though they were careful with their more dangerous magic because they didn't want to end up drawing unwanted attention.

"The dream was too vivid," Grandma pressed, unwilling to give up her side of the argument. "The more vivid they are, the more real they're likely to be."

"Where do you get your information?" I asked.

Grandma glared at me. "Are you going to act like the dream I had about your boyfriend wasn't real?"

I bristled. "I think it's weird that you would dream about my boyfriend under any circumstances." As much as I hated to admit it, though, she was right. When I was a teenager, Grandma had warned me that she'd had a dream about Tanner Hughes, my high school boyfriend, and Sassafras Persimmons. I'd ignored her to my detriment as I discovered on prom night.

"I was willing to put them in the burnbook," Grandma said, "but you were above that sort of thing if I recall."

I jerked my head toward her. "What burnbook?"

Her expression morphed into one of pure innocence. "Did I say a burnbook? I meant scrapbook."

I edged closer to her. "You said burnbook. I heard you." I could picture exactly the kind of burnbook my grandmother kept, full of perceived grievances and the hexes performed in retaliation.

"There's no burnbook, Eden," my mother said dismissively. "You know your grandmother."

"I do, which is why I want to see this book."

"There's no book," Grandma said. "I would never keep physical evidence of my crimes. Too risky." She paused. "I mean, alleged crimes."

I'd have to ask Neville if he could perform a locator spell on a burnbook. I shuddered to think what I'd find in there.

"Ryan, when are you going to figure out what you are and demonstrate your skills for Mom-mom?" my mother said in a sickeningly sweet voice.

I sat at the table and bit into my apple. "He's only a year old. Be patient."

My mother remained focused on her grandson. "He looks so much like Anton." She leaned forward. "Are you going to be a little vengeance demon like your daddy?"

Ryan smiled and bits of cheese fell out of his mouth.

"Well, he certainly eats like his daddy," Grandma said. She and Aunt Thora brought their cups of tea to the table.

"How's the training instructor?" Aunt Thora asked.

"Is he handsome?" my mother added.

I rolled my eyes. "Who cares? He's in town for two weeks."

"Two weeks is long enough," my mother said.

I shot her a quizzical look. "Long enough for what?"

"To make him fall in love with you," my mother said. "You're not getting any younger, you know."

"And you're not getting any smarter," Grandma said to her. "Eden isn't going to get involved with her instructor. That's not like her and you know it."

My mother harrumphed. "Seems like a missed opportunity to me."

"Every man you pass on the street seems like a missed opportunity to you," Grandma shot back.

"As much as I love a good bicker in the morning, I need to get going." I finished my apple and dumped the core in the bin.

"Will you be home for dinner?" Aunt Thora asked. "I was going to make cottage pie."

"I hope so," I said, "but my schedule is in the hands of Agent Redmond." For the next two weeks.

"Invite him to dinner," my mother said.

"No," I yelled over my shoulder and hurried from the house before anyone could hex me.

I met Agent Redmond on the sidewalk outside of The Daily Grind. Although he seemed skeptical of my claim that it was the only place for coffee in town, he didn't argue.

A gray haze seemed to have blanketed the morning sky. Visibility wasn't an issue, but it cast a dull shadow everywhere I looked.

"I thought the forecast said sunny for today," I said.

Agent Redmond looked skyward. "Reminds me of volcanic ash."

"Has there been an eruption somewhere?" I asked. "Maybe Iceland or Greenland?"

"Not to my knowledge," he replied.

My heart stuttered when I noticed a police cruiser coming toward us. The car slowed and I recognized the hunky silhouette of Chief Sawyer Fox in the driver's seat. If underwear models could moonlight as chiefs of police, that would be him. I was surprised to see another silhouette in the passenger seat beside him.

"Is that a dog?" Agent Redmond asked.

Sure enough, the car drew alongside us and the window rolled down to reveal an adorable Golden Retriever.

"Good morning, Officer," I said to the dog. "Are you on paw patrol?"

Chief Fox peered around the dog to smile at me. "This is Maximus."

Maximus punctuated the statement with a solid bark.

"Can I pet him?" I asked.

"That's why he's here," Chief Fox said.

I ran my hand through the dog's silky coat. "You mean he's not here to fight crime? Bummer."

"I'm hoping to get him adopted," Chief Fox said. "He's from the shelter. I read this article about police officers bringing dogs on patrol so that people might fall in love and adopt them. I thought it was a great idea."

Maximus panted. I understood the impulse. Chief Fox's abs of steel and heart of gold made me want to pant, too. Instead, I restrained myself and said, "Chief Fox, this is Agent Quinn Redmond from the FBI."

The chief's handsome face hardened. "Another agent? Is there a situation I should know about?" As far as the chief knows, I work for the cyber crime division of the FBI, investigating computer and network intrusions.

"No, no," I assured him. "We're old friends from San Francisco." I couldn't possibly tell Chief Fox the truth about Agent Redmond's visit. After all, secrecy was paramount. It was right there in rule number one.

Agent Redmond offered a pleasant smile. "Nice to meet you, Chief."

"Oh my goodness, look at that beautiful dog," a woman exclaimed. She practically mowed me down on the sidewalk to get to the car window.

"His name is Maximus," Chief Fox said. "He's available."

The woman beamed. "And how about his driver? Is he available, too?"

The chief chuckled. "I protect and serve, ma'am. No time for much else."

"You should make time." She rubbed her nose against the dog's. "And I would love to make time for this gorgeous fellow."

"I can make that easy for you," Chief Fox said. "Talk to Eileen at the Havarti Rescue Center."

17

The woman stepped away from the car. "Thank you so much, Chief. Keep up the good work." She turned and continued along the sidewalk.

The chief flashed a knowing smile. "See? Works like a charm."

"It's combined community service," I said. "Ingenious."

"You should see Deputy Guthrie," the chief said with a laugh. "He's not quite as comfortable with the idea as I am. The guy's never had a dog."

Somehow, I doubted Sean Guthrie even had a pet rock. Too much responsibility. The fact that he was the deputy in town still boggled my brain. We'd attended high school together and I wouldn't have trusted Sean to empty my trashcan, let alone provide law enforcement.

"What kind of dog does he have?" I asked.

"Today, it's a French bulldog named Fancy Nancy." The chief's sea-green eyes crinkled at the corners when he smiled and my legs wobbled a little in response.

Agent Redmond tapped the imaginary watch on his wrist. "We should keep moving, Agent Fury...Eden. Coffee's waiting."

I gave Maximum a final stroke. "Good luck, Maximus. I hope you find a forever home today."

The chief rolled up the window and drove away. I tore my gaze away from the car so that Agent Redmond didn't notice the longing in my eyes. It was silly, really. I barely knew the chief, yet I felt such a strong connection to him. Not that it mattered because getting involved with a human —and the chief of police, no less— was a very bad idea. He could never know my secret and I could never lie to someone I cared about. Best to keep a professional distance.

Before I opened the door to the coffee shop, I said, "Please be nice to everyone in here. I don't want anyone spitting in my latte."

"I'm unfailingly polite," Agent Redmond said.

I didn't doubt it.

The aroma of freshly brewed coffee filled my nostrils as we entered.

"Good morning, Eden," Caitlin said from behind the counter. "Your usual?"

"Yes, thanks." I inclined my head toward Agent Redmond. "And whatever this guy wants."

"I tend to avoid sugary carbs," Agent Redmond said. "I like to keep fit and healthy."

I could see that. "Pretend you're on vacation."

"I'm never on vacation, Agent Fury."

I could see that, too.

He leaned over the counter. "I'll have a large cinnamon macchiato with a double shot of espresso and a half pump of vanilla with original almond milk. No sugar added. Oh, and extra foam."

His order took me by surprise. I expected him to order a black coffee. I inched away from the agent and mouthed 'I'm sorry' to Caitlin.

"Didn't even need to twist your arm," I said.

Agent Redmond frowned. "I'm not even sure what I just ordered, to be honest."

Caitlin rang up our order and I paid.

"I thought that was you," a familiar voice said.

I turned to greet Clara Riley, my best friend. Her brown hair was styled in a single braid and her minimal makeup only served to accentuate her girl-next-door appeal.

"I'm a creature of habit." I shifted my gaze to Agent Redmond. "Clara, this is Quinn Redmond, a work colleague. He's in town for a couple weeks."

The uptight agent seemed momentarily caught off-guard. "Clara. What a beautiful name."

She gazed back at him. "Thank you. Your face is nice,

19

too." She squeezed her eyes closed. "I mean your name. Your name is nice."

Caitlin set our drinks on the counter. "Hope your day perks up!"

"Thank you," I said.

Clara tore her gaze away from Agent Redmond to look at me. "I bet that fog reminds you of San Francisco."

I smiled. "I had the same thought."

"I hope it doesn't get any worse or I won't want to drive," Clara said. "It'll be too hard to see."

"I have excellent vision," Agent Redmond said. "If you find yourself in a quandary, please don't hesitate to get in touch. I'll give you my number."

"Look at that," I said. "Quinn's a regular knight in brightly shining armor."

"Isn't he just?" Clara seemed smitten, which was highly unusual. As an empath, she tended to keep her distance from men and relationships. She typically found the experience too overwhelming and draining. I also suspected there was a little fear mixed in—that if the relationship soured, she wouldn't be able to handle the onslaught of emotion that often accompanied a breakup. Not that I blamed her. Breakups sucked.

"Would you like to join us?" Agent Redmond asked, surprising me yet again.

"I thought we were taking our drinks to the office," I said.

"I'd love to join you," Clara said, ignoring me.

"We'll be at the table by the window," Agent Redmond said.

I followed him to the table without a word. The fog outside seemed to be getting thicker by the minute.

Clara joined us a moment later. "Did you hear about the new coffee shop that's going to open?"

"No," I said.

"I saw the sign go up yesterday," Clara said. "It's called Magic Beans."

I sipped my latte. "I doubt it will be as good as here."

Clara leaned forward. "I heard through the grapevine that it's Corinne LeRoux's new venture."

"In that case, I'll never set foot in there." The LeRoux witches were a rival coven and the mere mention of their name in my house set my grandmother's teeth on edge. They originally came from Louisiana and were one of the first black families to settle in Chipping Cheddar. Adele, the matriarch, had a seat on the supernatural council. Her daughter, Rosalie, lacked her mother's sophisticated polish and ran a business further down on Asiago Street. Corinne was Adele's more elegant granddaughter and closer to my age. As much as I liked Corinne, I knew it was best to avoid her. Anything that annoyed my family was best avoided unless I wanted to end up dead in a ditch. I mean, they'd revive me, of course, but they might take their own sweet time about it.

"Tell me about yourself, Clara," Agent Redmond said. "Agent Fury tells me you're an empath."

I shushed him. "Rule number one, Agent Redmond."

He glowered at me. "No one is within earshot."

I glanced around the shop. Okay, fair point.

"I am," Clara said. "It's sort of like Eden's siphoning power, except I only deal with emotions."

"That must be challenging for you," he replied.

"I've learned to work around it," Clara said. "If I sense strong emotions emanating from someone, I make sure not to touch them."

"What a wondrous ability, though," he said. "To feel things so acutely."

"It has pros and cons," Clara said.

"Clara's a rising journalism star," I said. "She works for *The Buttermilk Bugle.*"

Agent Redmond seemed impressed. "Smart and beautiful. My favorite combination."

A blush crept into Clara's pale cheeks.

Sheesh. The icy, uptight agent from yesterday seemed to be thawing around my best friend. Maybe this unexpected development would help me get through the next two weeks.

Agent Redmond polished off his drink and looked at me. "Coffee break's over, Agent Fury. Time to get to work."

One could live in hope, anyway.

CHAPTER THREE

AFTER A SNOOZE-TASTIC MORNING spent reviewing protocol with Agent Redmond, I now sat at my desk paging through the daily report of supernaturals entering through North American portals from Otherworld while Agent Redmond grabbed lunch at the nearest salad bar.

"Are you doodling on the pictures of demons?" Neville asked, peering over my shoulder.

I flipped over the sheet of paper. "I don't know what you mean."

Neville slid the paper out from my beneath my hand and tapped the image. "You've drawn glasses and a mustache on that fire demon."

"It makes him look more distinguished, don't you think?" I snatched the paper back from him. "I doodle when I'm thinking. I can't help it."

"Maybe consider scrap paper?"

"Spoilsport. You're as uptight as Agent Redmond."

Neville straightened. "I resent that. I'm teeming with effervescence."

I stared at him. "That's too many big words in one small

23

sentence. You don't do that on dates, do you?" That could explain why he had so few of them.

Neville backed away. "I'll leave you to your reports, O caustic artistic one."

"Ooh, before I forget."

Neville froze. "Uh oh. What's your family done now?"

"What do you mean?"

He made a circle in the air with his finger. "You're wearing that face."

"I always wear this face. It's the only one I have."

"No, I mean the face you make when you're about to mention your family."

I picked up my phone and clicked open the mirror app to peer at my reflection. "I want to do a locator spell on a book that belongs to my grandmother." I set down the phone.

"A grimoire?" he asked.

"No, a burnbook."

He scrunched his nose. "I don't know what that is."

"That's because you're not a teenaged girl. Technically, it's like a diary where you talk smack about people. In writing."

"And your grandmother has such a thing?"

"I think so, except hers is magic-related," I said.

His brow lifted. "Ah, I see."

"I'd like to see a written record of her crimes and misdemeanors," I said. There were a few hexes I suspected her of but could never prove, including the time that tissues magically fell out of my shirt in the locker room at school. Everyone was convinced I was stuffing my bra and no amount of cleavage could convince them otherwise. I'd taken the last bagel that morning and remembered Grandma telling me it was fine. I should've known it wasn't fine. 'Fine' meant silently seething in our house.

"It would be helpful to have something of hers," Neville said.

I immediately produced a sealed plastic bag containing a few strands of Grandma's hair from her brush in the bathroom.

"I'll see what I can do."

Neville had just returned to his seat when the door opened and Agent Redmond appeared.

"Welcome back, Agent Redmond," Neville said.

"Lunchtime is over. I hope you're ready to resume," Agent Redmond said. "We have a busy afternoon ahead of us."

"What's on the agenda?" I asked. "Writing out each rule and regulation fifty times? Should Neville conjure a chalkboard?"

"Despite what you think, Agent Fury, this isn't a punishment," Agent Redmond said.

I glanced up at him. "So it only feels like one?"

He perched on the corner of my desk. "We'll start with a test."

My pulse began to race. "I thought the test was at the end of the two weeks."

"This one is a personality test," Agent Redmond said. "Myers-Briggs."

"I'm charming and committed to a fault," I said. "What more do they need to know?"

"It's a bit more scientific than that," he said, and directed me to the website.

I dutifully followed the instructions to start the test. "Why do they need this information? The FBI already has a thick file on me. I would think my personality is well-established by now."

"We prefer to do our own assessment in combination with the training program," Agent Redmond said. "The test won't take long and it won't hurt a bit."

"Tell that to my wrists," I said, rubbing them. "They're not used to all this typing."

Agent Redmond observed the screen over my shoulder. After a couple of minutes of feeling his breath on my shoulder, I twisted to look at him.

"Do you mind? Your breathing is distracting."

He begrudgingly moved to the other side of the office to bother Neville while I completed the questionnaire. Finally, the results were in.

"I'm an ENTJ, whatever that is," I said.

"The commander," Agent Redmond said. "Excellent."

"Is it? Sounds kind of militant." I didn't feel very militant.

Neville came hurrying over. "Oh, that's a good one. Where's there's a will, there's a way. That's your motto." He punched the air enthusiastically.

I craned my neck to look at him. "I have a motto?"

"Your personality does," Neville said.

"ENTJ's are natural born leaders," Agent Redmond said. "It's an ideal match for someone in this position."

"An FBM agent?" I asked.

"An agent in sole charge of a dormant portal," Agent Redmond said. "You'll be up for whatever challenge comes your way." He paused. "I hope."

"Because you'll use your ruthlessness and rational mind to achieve the goal you've set for yourself," Neville added.

I grimaced. "You make me sound like Hitler."

"Not to worry. Hitler was arguably an INFJ," Agent Redmond said.

A knock on the door made me jump.

"I'll get it." Neville hurried from his desk to make himself useful. "Oh, welcome Mrs. Fury."

"It's Beatrice," my mother said.

I cringed at the sound of my mother's voice. She knew better than to bother me at work. "Mom, what are you doing here?"

She entered the office holding a container of mixed nuts

"I can't get this open." She set the container on my desk and feigned surprise at Agent Redmond's presence. "I'm so sorry. How rude of me. I'm Beatrice Fury, Eden's incredibly young mother."

"Mom, I told you before about showing up at my office unannounced. I'm working."

"And this isn't?" She made a sweeping gesture toward the container. "I always bring these sort of tasks to Eden. She has the biggest hands in the family, you see. Matches her feet."

I bit my tongue. If she really wanted me to snag Agent Redmond, she needed to try a different tack.

"Bigger than Anton's?" Neville asked, genuinely curious.

"I wasn't counting the men," my mother said. "Though her father's feet are disappointingly small, just like..."

I coughed loudly. "Thank you, Mom."

"Anyway, I'm desperate for nuts." She took the opportunity to get a good look at Agent Redmond. "My, you really are one of the fair folk, aren't you?"

Agent Redmond's expression was neutral. "It's a pleasure to meet you, Mrs. Fury."

"Beatrice," my mother said with a coy smile. "That fog is so disruptive. I nearly ran a red light near Pimento Plaza because I couldn't see properly."

I unscrewed the lid and handed her the container. "Thanks for stopping by. Be careful driving back."

She clutched the container to her chest. "My hero." She sighed. "If only I had a man around to get into tight spots."

"It was a tight lid, Mom," I said. "No one's helping you with parallel parking."

She cocked an eyebrow. "Who said anything about parking?" She waved to Agent Redmond over her shoulder. "Hope to see you again soon."

I waited until the door closed and glanced at my assistant. "Neville, can you create a ward specific to my mother?"

27

Neville suppressed a smile. "I believe so."

"Good, then do it."

I returned my focus to Agent Redmond. "Now, where were we?"

"I'd like to see what you're capable of," he said.

"Well, you just saw what I can do with a container of mixed nuts."

"Yes, very impressive," he said. "We should take our training outside. The fog actually provides an excellent cover. No one will see us outside unless they're in close range."

"We can go to Davenport Park," I said. "I doubt anyone will be out walking when the visibility is so bad." Half the reason to go to the park was the view of the bay.

"Shall I accompany you?" Neville asked.

"No need, Mr. Wyman," Agent Redmond said.

"Hold down the fort, Neville," I said. "Keep an eye out for sophisticated fire demons with glasses and a smoking jacket."

"As you wish," he said.

Agent Redmond followed me to my car. "Let me know if you have trouble seeing through the fog. Fae are known for their keen vision."

"Thanks. My fog lights should be good enough."

We drove along the road that runs parallel to the bay. Usually I made a point of admiring the view, but there was no point today. The horizon was a blend of grays.

I parked the car adjacent to Davenport Park. As suspected, there was no one in sight.

"I guess you picked a good week to come," I said. "We don't need to rely on magic to hide our activities."

"We need a bit of space to work," he said.

We cut across the park and I heard the gurgle of the nearby river, although I couldn't see it through the haze.

28

"This is far enough," Agent Redmond said. "Now, I'd like a primer of your abilities. Where should we start?"

I mulled over the options. "I'm fast and strong."

He stifled a laugh. "Yes, I believe your mother established your strength."

I glared at him. "She likes to attribute it to my big hands and pretends it has nothing to do with my fury powers."

"And she's a witch?"

"The most wicked kind," I said. The words slipped out before I could stop them. I had no intention of discussing my family in detail with Agent Redmond. I didn't want to raise any red flags with the FBM.

"How wicked?" he asked.

"It doesn't matter," I said, knowing very much that it did.

"Your file says that your father is a vengeance demon."

"Non-practicing," I lied. "He prefers golf to revenge."

Agent Redmond regarded me. "I'm beginning to understand you a little better."

That didn't sound like a compliment.

"Pretend I'm a demon that's escaped through the portal," he said. "Show me what you would do."

"I can't do that."

"Of course you can." He smiled. "I have abilities of my own, Agent Fury. You won't hurt me."

"It isn't that."

"Here, I'll make it easier." Agent Redmond pulled a small pouch from his pocket and sprinkled colorful dust in the air between us. "Subdue this standard issue demon."

A bright orange bug-eyed demon stood between us. The creature was short and stout with a reptilian tail. He locked eyes with me and opened his jaws wide.

I stared at him blankly. "I don't know what to do."

"Use the Force, Luke," Agent Redmond advised.

"Ha. You're hilarious." A joke from Agent Redmond? Whatever next?

Agent Redmond stepped through the illusion of the demon. "Usually, I have to rein agents in. They want to show off their skills like it's the Westminster Supernatural Show."

I perked up. "Did you see the dog that won this year? Sweet Hecate, he was the most adorable thing ever."

Agent Redmond snapped his fingers. "Focus, Agent Fury, and stop trying to distract me with thoughts of cute puppies. It won't work."

"You brought it up!"

"I made an analogy." He squared his shoulders. "Let's try this again." He moved aside so that I had a full view of the demon again.

"I can't attack him when I know he isn't real," I said.

"Use your imagination."

I made a halfhearted effort to punch the orange demon.

Agent Redmond tugged the ends of his short hair in frustration. "No, this won't work. What's your most impressive power?"

I shrugged. "I don't know. I guess my new wings."

"Wings? You can fly?" He seemed taken aback.

"I need to practice more but, arguably, yes." If the wind blew in the right direction, I could coast without hurting myself.

He gave a quick shake of his head in disbelief. "Then you can attack this demon from above. Why bother to meet him on his level, Agent Fury? Use your advantage."

"I don't want to." I knew I sounded ridiculously stubborn, but I didn't care.

Agent Redmond snapped his fingers and the illusion dispersed. "Clearly, I need to approach this a different way."

"By just signing off on my training and calling it a day? Terrific. I'm on board."

He ignored me. "You've seen *Dirty Dancing*, yes?"

"Only if you're referring to the original film with Patrick Swayze and Jennifer Grey," I replied.

He frowned. "Is there any other version?"

Finally, something we agreed on.

"I'd like you to picture yourself as Baby Houseman," he said.

"Are we in the Catskills?"

"We're anywhere you want to be, as long as you're in the right mindset."

I closed my eyes and conjured a mental image. "Okay, I've just told my parents that I'm going to change the world and Anton is going to decorate it."

"Anton is your brother?"

I nodded.

"Great. Fast forward to the lift."

My eyes snapped open. "The lift? But we haven't even gotten to the dancing montage."

He pointed to the ground. "This *is* the dancing montage, Agent Fury. We're running through your abilities, or trying to."

Less effectively than Baby and Johnny Castle, it seemed.

"Think of using your wings as leaping into Johnny's arms as he lifts you into the air for the big finish." He raised his arms above his head.

My throat tightened. "I don't want to do the lift."

He crossed his arms and peered at me. "Why not? Baby's scared, but she pushes through in the end."

"Because Baby didn't risk turning evil through the magic of dance."

He sighed in exasperation. "You're not a Furby. You're not going to turn evil."

"I'm only one letter off," I insisted.

He was silent for a moment. "I think this might take more than two weeks."

My hands moved to my hips. "Have you ever worked with a fury before, Agent Redmond?"

"No, furies are among the rarest supernaturals."

"Then you don't understand."

"I understand that you have amazing abilities that you refuse to use, even for the sake of helping others. If you ask me, that's only a few rungs down on the evil ladder."

"The more I use them, the more the fury part of me takes over," I said. "Yes, I might save a few kittens from trees along the way, but at what price in the long run? I have to stay focused on the forest and not the trees...or kittens contained therein."

Agent Redmond blinked. "Is there an actual kitten epidemic in this town that I should know about?"

My hands dropped to my sides. "No, but there could be. Who would know with all this fog?"

He clenched his fists into balls. "Agent Fury, work with me, please. You're an agent for the Federal Bureau of Magic. This job requires that you engage with your supernatural side. There's no choice."

"I know. That's why I didn't want to work for them."

"And so you went to the FBI instead?"

"I want to help people, but not with my powers."

"But it's foolish to ignore such gifts," he said. "You're allowing your fear of the unknown to control to you."

"No, I'm letting the fear of the known control me," I said. "I grew up in a house full of dark magic and revenge and I have fought against it with every fiber of my being."

"Then you have very little to worry about," Agent Redmond said. "The fact that you're self-aware is a huge step in the right direction."

"Self-aware doesn't equal self-control."

Agent Redmond paced in front of me. "You do realize that this training program ends with a simulation exercise where you'll have no choice but to use your powers, yes?"

My shoulders sagged. "Fine. Bring back the bug-eyed demon."

"Excellent. I knew you were a team player, Agent Fury."

"Just out of curiosity, what if I don't pass?"

"My agents don't fail, Agent Fury," he said. "If we work together to the best of our abilities, then you'll pass."

"I'll pass," I repeated.

But what if I didn't want to?

CHAPTER FOUR

I ARRIVED home with aching muscles and a sour attitude after a long day with Agent Redmond. Our dancing montage included far more feats of strength and speed than I'd originally planned to showcase. He was good at his job, I'd give him that much.

My mother intercepted me before I reached the kitchen. "I need you to review this letter for me." She whipped a folded sheet of paper toward me.

I took the letter. "Why do I need to read this for you? Did Grandma make you illiterate again?" That was not a fun day.

"No, it's from the HOA and it's confusing."

"I'm not a lawyer. You should give it to Uncle Moyer."

My mother waved a dismissive hand. "Oh, you know your uncle. He's so stodgy about everything."

My eyes narrowed to slits. "You said that I was wound tighter than a spool of thread."

"Oh, Eden. Why can't you let things go? That was ages ago."

"It was yesterday." I scanned the letter. "The HOA says you're in violation of rule 59(a)(1)."

"Which rule is that?"

"How should I know?" I continued to read. "Ah, the one that says you must remove any holiday decorations after three days."

"Three days? That's outrageous."

I shrugged and handed her back the letter. "What decorations are they talking about?" I hadn't noticed any.

"Alban Eilir," my mother said. "We celebrated at your sister-in-law's request."

"The Light of the Earth?" I'd never celebrated it, but I knew it was the point where light and darkness were considered once again in balance. A time of new beginnings.

"Yes, she wants Olivia and Ryan to enjoy some of the druid holidays. I wasn't in favor, but I didn't want to make a fuss."

"Since when?"

My mother shoved the letter in her pocket. "I guess someone complained about the black and white ribbon on the mailbox."

"*That's* your decoration?"

"I let Olivia tie it there. She was so excited." She smiled. "Wait until I tell Anton about this. He'll find out who complained and then they'll be sorry."

"Please don't," I said. "Especially not while Agent Redmond is in town."

Her lips melted into a smile. "He's very attractive."

I moved past her. "You can stop talking now." I found the rest of my family in the kitchen.

"We thought you got lost in the mist," Aunt Thora said. She removed a rectangular pan from the oven and set it on a trivet.

"It isn't mist, it's fog," Anton said. "It took me twice as long to get home as normal. The cars are crawling."

"There's something wrong with this fog," Grandma said from her place at the table.

"Is there anything you don't criticize?" my mother asked. "Why don't you criticize the sun for burning just a smidge too hot? Or the grass for being too green?"

"Depends on the lawn," Grandma said. "Husbourne Crawley's grass isn't green enough. I'm pretty sure he invites the werewolves over to pee on it in the dark."

"Grandma! He does not," I said. "Why would you even say that?" Husbourne Crawley was far too Southern and genteel to do such a thing. He also served on the supernatural council *and* the regular town council, which made him prone to stick to rules—and public urination by werewolves would violate more than one of them.

"I don't like the fog either," Verity chimed in. My sister-in-law glanced uneasily at her children. "It makes me uncomfortable. I don't even want the children to play outside."

"They'll be fine," my mother said. "They don't have any respiratory problems. All you need to do is hear them yell to know that. Good lungs, both of them."

"I'm not concerned about their breathing," Verity replied. "I'm worried about them disappearing."

"Verity's right," Anton said. "The fog seems to be getting thicker by the day. The weather app just shows a gray smudge on the map where our town should be."

"San Francisco had its share of fog, but this does have a different feel to it," I said.

"How's your supervisor?" Grandma asked.

I bristled. "He's not my supervisor. Agent Redmond is a training instructor."

"Is he handsome?" Aunt Thora asked.

"Very," my mother said.

"I heard he and Clara hit it off," Grandma said.

"Who told you that?" I asked. I'd deliberately not

mentioned their meeting in the coffee shop because I knew it would attract attention.

"Anton told us," Grandma replied.

I shot my brother a reproachful look. He knew perfectly well that I didn't want to share personal details with my mother or Grandma. Nothing that could be used against me.

"I only mentioned it in passing," Anton said.

"You weren't supposed to mention it at all," I shot back.

My mother fingered her necklace. "I could help you win him over, you know. No point letting a human get her hooks into him."

I waved my hands. "No, absolutely not. I'm not interested."

"You're making a mistake passing on that one, Eden." My mother shivered with delight. "Fae like him can curl a woman's hair."

Verity gave her a sharp look. "Can we not discuss such things at the dinner table?"

My mother leveled her with a cool gaze. "Where should we discuss it then? The place where only the adults lounge? Oh, wait. We can't have adults only conversations until you *move out.*"

Anton seemed to sense the unrest building. "The contractor said things are moving along, but the fog has slowed them down."

My mother groaned. "Of course it has."

"What about John?" Verity asked. "Is he still working on the barn?"

"Not today," I said. "He texted me that he thought it would be too dangerous and said he'd come back when it clears."

"Well, this is unacceptable," my mother said. "The fog is making a mess of everything."

"It's also slowing down my training," I said. "If it keeps up, Agent Redmond will need to stay longer."

That nugget seemed to lift her spirits. "Well, I suppose there's nothing we can do about it. Might as well enjoy it while it lasts."

"I want to go outside for recess, but we're not allowed," Olivia complained.

I only made it halfway through dinner when Frank Sinatra's *Fly Me To The Moon* blasted from my phone.

"No phones at the table," my mother said sharply.

"It's Julie," I said. Julie is a werewolf married to my cousin Rafael, a warlock. My family wasn't too sure about welcoming a werewolf into the family, but Julie proved to be a family favorite over time, even winning over my mother's side of the family—no small feat.

"Eden, there's a problem with Meg."

I tensed at the sound of Julie's frantic voice. "What's wrong?"

"She's been arrested," Julie said. "Will you go down to the station?"

"Arrested? For what?"

"Who's been arrested?" my mother asked. Suddenly the presence of a phone at the table wasn't an issue.

Julie broke down and sobbed. "I don't know."

I frowned into the phone. "You don't know?"

"I'm on my way there now," she said. "Chief Fox called and said Meg had been arrested. I thought it might help if you were there, being a federal agent."

"Of course. I'll head right over." I picked up my plate and brought it to the counter. "I need to go to the station. Meg's been arrested." I couldn't imagine what the sixteen-year-old could've done. Meg wasn't prone to bad behavior. Her genes favored Julie, not my wretched family.

"Should I call Moyer?" Aunt Thora asked.

38

"Let me see what's going on first," I said. Chief Fox seemed as reasonable as he was hot. Hopefully there'd be no need to get lawyers involved.

The small parking lot at the police station was blocked off for construction, so I parked on the street two blocks away and sprinted to the building.

"Really? You're the cavalry?" Deputy Sean Guthrie lingered in the lobby beside the receptionist's desk.

"Really? You're the deputy?" Sean and I had one thing in common—a mutual dislike of each other.

The redhead tapped the badge on his shirt. "You're in my house now, Eden. Respect the badge."

I folded my arms. "I've got my own badge and it didn't come out of a cereal box."

"Why don't you go back to your computer? That's where all the action is for you anyway."

"What's the difference between a redhead and vampire?" I asked. I didn't bother to wait for a response. "One is a soulless, bloodsucker that's too pale for the sun." I paused for a beat. "The other is a vampire."

Sean clenched his jaw. "That doesn't even make sense because vampires aren't real," he shot back.

"What's the most unrealistic thing in the Harry Potter films?"

"Duh. That Voldemort could breathe with that nose. Everybody knows that."

"Wrong. It's that a redheaded kid managed to have two friends."

"You're one to talk. The only friend you ever had was Clara."

A sharp whistle grabbed my attention. Chief Fox stood in the doorway of his office. "When you're done harassing my deputy, maybe you'd like to step inside and discuss your cousin's arrest."

My face warmed and I knew my cheeks had to be the color of tomatoes. "Of course." I brushed past Sean, ignoring his smirk.

"Very mature," Chief Fox said in a low voice.

"What can I say? He brings it out in me," I replied.

He closed the door behind us. Julie and Meg were already seated next to each other. I noticed that Meg held her mother's hand.

"You okay?" I asked Meg.

The sixteen-year-old nodded. "It's a misunderstanding."

"You mean you didn't take anything?" I asked. There wasn't a third chair so I continued to stand and tried not to appear judgy while looming over my cousin.

"She took a phone from Bullseye," Chief Fox said. "The security guard caught her."

Meg looked ready to burst into tears. Her red eyes told me she already had, at least once.

"A phone?" I repeated. "Meg, you don't have a phone."

"I guess that's why she decided to steal one," the chief said.

I shook my head. "No, you don't understand. Meg doesn't have a phone because she doesn't want one."

"I've been trying to explain that," Julie said. "I would very much like her to have a phone and I'm more than willing to buy one for her, but she refuses to own one."

Chief Fox appeared perplexed. "Let me get this straight. The teenager is arguing with a parent because she doesn't want a phone?"

"Yes," Meg said. "Technology is taking over our lives. I prefer to be present in the moment."

"And I prefer to know you're not dead in a ditch," Julie replied.

Meg rolled her eyes. "Mom. There are very few ditches in Chipping Cheddar."

"Can we get back to the real issue?" Chief Fox asked. "Meg, if you don't want a phone, why did you steal one?"

Meg chewed her lip. "Because...I don't know. It called to me. It wanted me to take it."

"Phones don't speak, honey," Julie said. "Well, unless someone calls you on it. Did someone call and you answered it?"

"No," Meg said. "It just caught my eye and, before I knew it, I'd put it in my bag."

"Taking an item you don't need sounds like kleptomania," I said.

"Taking an item you don't own sounds like theft," the chief argued.

I fixed him with a hard stare. "Chief, listen to her. She didn't steal because of greed or to make money. She stole something she doesn't need."

"Maybe she intended to sell it," Chief Fox said.

"We have plenty of money," Julie said, visibly annoyed. "My husband owns Chophouse. It's the most successful restaurant in town."

"A cry for attention then?" the chief asked. "Maybe Meg is being ignored at home with two busy parents?"

I focused on Meg. It was possible, although I always got the impression that Julie was a doting mother—a common werewolf trait.

"I don't know what came over me," Meg said, her voice quivering. "I didn't think. I saw the phone and I took it. I don't know how else to explain it. I'm really sorry."

A cry erupted and I realized it was Julie, not Meg. "This is awful," she blurted.

"It'll be okay, Mom," Meg said, in an effort to comfort her.

"I try to raise you in spite of your genes," Julie wailed.

I understood the sentiment.

"Meg is an excellent student with no history of bad behavior," I said. "Not even a detention. Can we talk about letting her off with a warning?"

Chief Fox glanced from a crying Julie to me. "We can talk about it."

Meg shot to her feet. "I'd be so grateful, Chief. I swear I'll never do it again."

"We'll put you on probation," Chief Fox said. "Any more incidents like this and I'll have to reconsider."

"Yes, of course." Meg's head bobbed up and down. "You'll never see me again, not in this capacity anyway."

Julie wiped away tears with the back of her hand. "Thank you, Chief. Your mercy won't be forgotten." She placed an arm around her daughter and guided her out of the office.

I lingered for a moment longer.

"Something you want to say, Agent Fury?"

"Thank you," I said. "You won't regret this."

"To be honest, she's not the first case of a good kid gone wrong I've seen today. Must be something in the water."

My brow lifted. "Another shoplifting case?"

He looked thoughtful. "Sort of. A young guy stole a bottle of wine from one of the restaurants along the waterfront."

I balked. "He stole wine from a restaurant?"

"He was there with his parents," the chief said. "They were about to leave when he walked straight to the back room and tried to walk out with the wine." He scratched the back of his neck. "His parents were mortified."

"What about him?"

"He was like Meg. No history of bad behavior. He said himself he doesn't even like wine."

"Then why did he take it?"

"Because he wanted to see if he could," Chief Fox said.

"Sounds like a fraternity prank."

"The fog's been keeping us busy enough with minor accidents," the chief said. "I don't need a spate of petty crimes on top of it. I even had to arrest a woman on domestic violence charges today." He shook his head. "She was so shaken up. She seemed like the type to trap spiders in the glass and release them in the garden, you know?"

I did know. I *was* that type.

"How's Maximus?" I asked. "Any takers?"

He broke into a grin at the mention of the dog. "Yes, thanks for asking. I'd like to do more, but I need to wait until the fog lifts. I've gotten too busy to stop and chat with people."

We stood in awkward silence for a moment. The conversation was clearly over, yet neither of us made a move to leave.

"Purple's a nice color for you," he finally said. "Brings out your eyes."

I glanced down at my top. "Thank you. Your badge makes your chest sparkle." I winced as soon as the words left my mouth. What did I just say? It didn't even make sense.

Thankfully, we were interrupted by the ring of the chief's phone. He snatched it to his ear. "Chief Fox." He listened intently. "I'll be right there." He clicked off the phone and looked at me. "I'm sorry. Duty calls."

Reluctantly, I turned to leave. "I understand," I said.

All too well.

CHAPTER FIVE

As I walked the two blocks to my car, I replayed the moment over in my mind, cringing every step of the way. *Your badge makes your chest sparkle?* It was worse than Baby Houseman telling Johnny that she carried a watermelon.

I heard a noise ahead and peered through the fog.

"Hey, that's my car!" Someone was seated in the front seat. I couldn't believe how brazen the thief was. The car was only two blocks from the police station.

I sprinted to the car before he could hot wire it and drive away. His face registered shock when I banged on the window. Super speed was the most I was willing to risk. It was easy to convince people I was simply very fast.

I yanked open the car door before he could lock it. "Get out," I said.

The young man paled. "I didn't know it was yours."

"But you knew it wasn't yours, which seems to be the critical fact."

The would-be thief slid out of the driver's seat. "I don't know what came over me. I...I'm sorry. I really need a set of wheels."

44

"Try a bike," I said. "They're cheaper."

He seemed dazed and confused. "I've never stolen a car before."

"And you still haven't," I said, "but only because I got here in time."

"Please don't have me arrested," he said. "It'll ruin my chance for a college scholarship. I'm supposed to play lacrosse next year."

"What's your name?"

"Benny. Benny McCoy."

"I'll tell you what Benny McCoy," I said. "I know your name and what you look like. I'm feeling generous, so I'll keep this little incident between us." Only because the chief had done the same for Meg.

Relief washed over his face. "Thank you so much," he said.

I held up a finger. "I'm not finished yet. If I hear that you so much as took a lollipop from the bank without asking, I will find you. And trust me when I tell you that I won't be so lenient next time."

Benny nodded profusely. "I won't. I promise." He ran off and disappeared into the fog before I could change my mind.

I was about to get into the car when the glow of red lights cut through the haze. I scowled when I caught sight of Sean in the driver's seat of the police car. I'd already had my fill of the deputy today.

Sean pulled his car behind mine. "Everything okay here, Fury?" he asked.

"Does everything look okay?"

He glanced at my car and back to me. "I guess so. There's been an uptick in criminal activity. The chief just went to check out a break-in. He thinks people are getting a little stir crazy from the fog."

"I'm getting the same vibe," I said.

"Someone tried to break the window of the electronics store last night. Did the chief tell you?"

"Looting?" I asked. That seemed out of character for the town and for the occasion. It wasn't as though a hurricane had blown through and most of the residents had evacuated. Everyone was here.

"That's what the chief is worried about," Sean said. "Well, one of the things he's worried about. Maybe you could make yourself useful and offer to patrol a section of town."

I was taken aback. Sean actually wanted my help? "You think I'd be useful?"

"More useful than sitting in front of a computer playing solitaire."

I eyed him closely. "It wasn't your idea, was it?"

He scowled. "What's the difference?"

I laughed. "Chief Fox told you to find me before I left, didn't he?" And now Sean was trying to pass it off as his own idea. Typical.

Sean ignored me. "Why don't you take the north end of town?"

"Now?"

"Unless you have other plans."

"No problem," I said. "I'll call the chief if I have any issues."

"Call me," Sean said. "I'll tell the chief."

I got into my car. "Sure thing." There was no point in arguing. I'd just do what I wanted anyway.

I joined the road, creeping along with my fog lights on. It was difficult enough to watch for other vehicles, but I was also concerned about pedestrians and animals. They didn't come equipped with fog lights.

I reached an intersection and waited for the light to turn green. A mother stood at the corner with one child in a stroller and another by her side holding a ball. I thought it

46

was a little late to be out with two small kids, but it wasn't my business. Maybe she worked off hours and had picked them up from daycare.

The light changed and, as I stepped on the gas pedal, the child on foot lost his hold on the ball and darted into the street to retrieve it.

"Justin!" the mother screamed.

I hit the brake and swerved to avoid hitting him.

Justin bent down to retrieve his ball and ran back to his mother, crying.

I rolled down my window. "Is he okay?"

The mother gripped Justin by the arm. "I can't believe he did that. He knows better." She looked at Justin. "You know better!"

"My ball," Justin said, and exploded into tears again.

The car behind me honked and I drove on, slightly rattled. That was a close call. I was lucky my reflexes were faster than normal. Actually, Justin was lucky my reflexes were faster than normal.

I drove at a low speed as I passed Davenport Park. I peered into the fog for any signs of trouble. If there was an uptick in criminal activity, then it wouldn't surprise me if there were troublemakers here.

I decided to check out the area on foot. I parked the car and walked across the street to the mound, the hillside where the dormant portal was hidden from view. I figured I might as well check the portal while I was here and make sure everything was as it should be.

I felt the pulsating energy emanating from the portal. The energy seemed no more mystical than usual.

I placed my hands on the rock formations. "Yep. Still dormant," I said.

I exited the mound and was immediately enveloped in fog once again. I could barely see a foot in front of me.

Hedwig's Theme began to play and I pulled my phone from my pocket. "Everything okay, Neville?"

"There was a domestic violence incident reported earlier," he said. "Miriam Travers. A neighbor called when they saw her beating her husband in the front yard with a rolling pin."

I stopped walking. "People still use rolling pins?"

"Not the point, Agent Fury."

"Why would I get involved in a domestic dispute?"

"From what I've heard, the incident is out of character for Mrs. Travers."

I remembered Chief Fox making a similar remark at the police station. "The fog is taking a toll," I said. "People are getting antsy."

"You think Mrs. Travers beat her husband because she was feeling antsy? Seems extreme."

"You think there might be something supernatural at work?"

"Worth a brief conversation," Neville said. "Don't you think?"

"What I think is that I'd like to go home, get in my pajamas, and watch TV with Alice."

"Are you certain you want to risk overlooking a supernatural incident while Agent Redmond is in town?" Neville asked.

Argh. He made a good point. "Fine," I huffed. "Who reported the incident? I'll see what I can find out."

"Her name is Jane Turnbull." He gave me the address.

"Thanks." As ready as I was to veg out with Alice in front of the television, I knew I couldn't ignore a potential supernatural incident. Not with Agent Redmond here ticking his training boxes. I'd probably be in violation of multiple rules without even realizing it.

Fighting feelings of resentment, I got back in my car and headed southwest.

. . .

It was pitch dark when I pulled into the driveway. I was surprised to see Mrs. Turnbull on her front porch, sweeping off the dirt. She stopped when she saw me approach and set aside the broom. "Can I help you?"

"Jane Turnbull?"

"That's me."

"I'm Agent Eden Fury." I flashed my badge. To the untrained human eye, it looked like an FBI badge. To any supernaturals, it showed that I was an agent of the Federal Bureau of Magic. "I'd like to speak to you about your neighbors if you have a minute."

"I have lots of minutes thanks to this ridiculous fog," she replied. "I don't want to leave the house to go anywhere, unlike my husband, who sees it as an excuse to spend more time at the country club." She opened the front door and gestured for me to come inside.

The first thing I noticed about the interior was the owner's obsession with owls. There were owls in the wallpaper design, owl figurines in a curio cabinet, and even the image of an owl etched in the wool rug on the foyer floor.

"You must really like owls," I remarked.

Mrs. Turnbull blinked her large eyes at me. "What makes you say that?"

She continued into the living room and offered me a drink. I declined and sat in the worn leather chair that faced the fireplace.

"I understand you're the one who reported the incident next door," I said.

Mrs. Turnbull's features were etched with concern. "Such a strange day it's been."

"Can you tell me exactly what happened?"

She grabbed a blanket from the back of the sofa and

draped it over her shoulders. "I'm chilly one minute and sweating the next. It happens to women my age. Something for you to look forward to."

I wasn't sure whether furies experienced menopause. Maybe there was actually something good about being a fury after all.

"The whole incident was shocking," Mrs. Turnbull said. "I was on the porch watering the plants when I heard shouting. Miriam has never so much as raised her voice to call him for supper, but she was raging."

"Could you understand what she was saying?" I asked.

"Yes and no. She used quite a lot of swear words I was surprised she even knew," Mrs. Turnbull said. "I've only heard my husband use words like that when he's hurt himself."

"I see."

"I went to the end of the porch and, there she was on the front lawn, pounding on him with a rolling pin like he was a chicken cutlet."

"Did you intervene?" I asked.

"Absolutely not," Mrs. Turnbull said. "I came inside and called the police. I feel horrible about it, but I didn't know what else to do." She clutched the blanket. "I've been watching the house and she hasn't come home yet. I'm going to bake them an apple pie."

"Did they seem happily married before today?" I asked.

She snorted. "No idea. What does happily married even look like anymore?"

"You said she didn't typically yell, but did they argue?"

"Not that I ever heard," Mrs. Turnbull said. "They seem to get along really well for being married as long as they have."

"Any recent visitors to the house?" I asked. I was trying to think of some kind of supernatural influence but was coming up empty.

Mrs. Turnbull plucked an imaginary thread on the blanket. "No, not that I saw." She heaved a sigh. "Miriam is such a nice woman. I wish I hadn't called the police. I just reacted, you know?"

"You shouldn't feel guilty," I said. "You did what you thought was best."

Mrs. Turnbull fixed her gaze on the details of the blanket. More owls, of course. "I was too nervous to intervene myself, but I was worried she'd kill him. One good knock on the head could have done it."

"I appreciate your help," I said. "And I'm sure Mr. Travers does, too."

I rose to my feet and Mrs. Turnbull escorted me to the door. "We used to alternate pot luck dinners, but I suspect that's not going on next month's calendar."

I walked back to the sidewalk and decided to proceed up the walkway to the Travers' house. I was already here, so there was no harm in digging a little deeper.

Simon Travers answered the door, dressed in sweatpants and a faded black T-shirt. His chin was covered in white stubble and he had a black eye and an angry bruise on his cheek.

"Aren't you a little old to be selling Girl Scout Cookies?" he asked.

Now *I* wanted to hit him with a rolling pin. Instead, I showed him my badge. "My name is Agent Eden Fury. Can I please come in?"

His brow creased. "The FBI is interested in a marital spat?"

"Let's talk inside," I said.

He widened the gap so I could enter. "It was an argument that got out of hand. That's it. We weren't ourselves."

I stepped into the foyer. "Weren't yourselves? Were there drugs involved?"

He recoiled. "Drugs? Are you kidding?"

"Is that so shocking? People of all ages engage in drug use, Mr. Travers."

"I guess that explains why the FBI is interested," he said. "The only people using recreational drugs at my age are ones with a death wish. That's heart attack city right there."

Although the layout of his house was identical to Mrs. Turnbull's house, the interior was vastly different. No owl in sight, but plenty of nature photographs in frames on the wall. Waterfalls, sunsets, scenic valleys.

"You like to travel, Mr. Travers?" I asked.

His eyes darted to the photos. "Yes, my wife in particular."

"She took those photos? They're beautiful."

"Oh, no. Those are aspirational. Places she wants to go when we retire." His expression clouded over. "I don't suppose you're allowed to have a drink."

He padded into the kitchen and I noticed the bottle of whiskey on the counter. A half-filled glass sat beside it.

"No, but I won't stop you from finishing yours."

"Good." He swiped the glass from the counter and downed the brown liquid. "It's been that kind of week."

"When you said neither of you acted like yourselves, can you explain what you meant?"

Mr. Travers poured himself more whiskey. "Well, for starters, my wife is very docile," he said. "She's never had a temper. Even when I crashed our car on the way to our honeymoon, she didn't say a word other than to make sure I wasn't hurt."

"I heard she whacked you with a rolling pin."

His hand went instinctively to touch the bruise on his cheek. "I deserved every lick."

"What did you do, if you don't mind me asking?"

His gaze lowered. "I spent money I shouldn't have."

I cast a quick glance around the house, looking for

evidence of a big splurge. The only car in the driveway was an older model Toyota and I didn't see anything expensive inside the house.

"On what?" I asked.

He fidgeted with his glass. "On nothing worthwhile. I gambled it and lost."

Ouch. "Was it a lot of money?"

"Our retirement savings," he mumbled.

For a second, I thought I hadn't heard him correctly. "Did you say you blew through your retirement savings gambling?"

"A private poker game," he said. "I don't even know what possessed me to go. My friends from the senior center go to this house every week to play and I always say no. For whatever reason, I said yes this week. I'm still not sure why I changed my mind."

"That's a pretty high stakes poker game if you lost your retirement savings."

He thrust out his hands. "I don't know what got into me. I knew Miriam would be apoplectic. It took us ages to save all that money and she was desperate to travel. She's been looking forward to it for years."

Now I understood why he looked upset when I drew attention to the nature photos. Miriam wouldn't get the chance to visit any of those places without the money they'd saved.

"Was someone pressuring you into betting?" I asked. I'd have to look into the host of the poker games. He could be a supernatural con artist and influencing the outcome.

"Only the voice in my head." He downed the rest of his drink and looked at me. "I mean my own voice, not someone else's."

"Have you had issues with gambling in the past?" I asked.

"When I was younger, I liked to bet," he said, "but it was a condition of the marriage that I had to stop, so I did."

"A condition?" I asked.

"Miriam and I had dated long enough for her to realize that money would slip through my fingertips like water. She laid down the law when I proposed."

"And you've stuck to it all this time until now?"

His head bobbed up and down. "We had two kids. Put them through college. Scrimped and saved and then I blew it all in one day." He ran his hand over his face. "I'm still surprised she didn't shove that rolling pin up my..."

I held up a hand. "Thank you, Mr. Travers. I get the picture."

"She's a good woman," he said. "She doesn't deserve to be punished for what she did."

"I'm sorry, Mr. Travers."

"So am I. More than I can ever express. Once I started playing, it was like all those old feelings came back."

"From when you used to gamble?"

He ran his thumb around the rim of the glass. "I guess I was chasing a different kind of high."

"What's the name of the host for these poker games?" I asked.

Mr. Travers seemed reluctant to answer. "It's confidential," he finally said.

"I promise I won't go barging in there with my badge on display," I said. "I just want to sniff around and make sure he's not cheating people." And make sure he's human.

"The whole thing is illegal, though, right? I don't want you to make an arrest. They'll know I'm the snitch and everyone at the senior center will hate me. They look forward to poker nights."

"I'll be discreet," I said. "I promise."

He sucked in air. "Okay, the host is Jaclyn Brewster."

"Jaclyn?" For some reason, I expected the host to be a man. Some feminist I was.

"Yeah. Nice lady. Everybody likes her." Mr. Travers dragged a hand through his thinning hair. "Ugh. This week has already been the worst. I don't need everyone else to hate me on top of my wife." His face grew anguished. "You're a woman. Do you think she'll ever forgive me?"

"I really don't know, Mr. Travers," I said. "Even if she loves you enough, that's a bitter pill to swallow."

He put the empty glass on the counter. "I want to take her to all those places she's dreamed of going to. It isn't fair that she should suffer for my stupid mistake."

I clapped him on the shoulder. "It'll be okay, Mr. Travers." I honestly had no idea if that was true, but it seemed like the right thing to say.

"I hope so," he said. "We have a good marriage. All these years, I managed to keep my gambling in check. I'd hate to throw it away now."

I thought of my own parents and the dissolution of their marriage. It hadn't been one huge mistake, but rather lots of small disagreements. Seemingly insignificant fissures in the relationship that cracked and widened over time. If the Travers had a solid marital foundation, I felt confident they'd make it.

"Good luck, Mr. Travers."

"Hey, you're FBI," he said. "Can you talk to anyone about letting Miriam off the hook? Maybe you have a special relationship with the police chief?"

A special relationship.

I thought of my brief time alone with Chief Fox in his office earlier and my stomach fluttered. "I'll see what I can do."

CHAPTER SIX

I WAS ONLY a mile from home when a call came through on the Bluetooth.

"Where are you?" Clara's voice burst through the speakers.

"Where are you?" I could barely hear her with the background noise.

"Cheese Wheel," she yelled. "Come and play."

"I'm tired. I don't think a night of drinking is in the cards for me."

"Then don't drink," Clara said. "Just observe. It's amazing people watching tonight. You have no idea."

Now I was intrigued. "What kind of people watching?"

"Nope. You have to come and see for yourself."

I debated my options. Part of me wanted nothing more than to be in pajamas snuggled under the covers. The other part of me wanted to have a good time with my best friend.

Ultimately, fun won out and I turned the car in the direction of The Cheese Wheel.

The parking lot was surprisingly full for a weeknight. I

entered the bar and was greeted with an even bigger surprise.

"Agent Redmond?" The uptight agent was the last person I expected to see knocking back drinks at The Cheese Wheel.

He seemed equally startled to see me. "Agent Fury, good evening."

It was only then that I noticed Clara stood beside him. Very close beside him, in fact.

"Oh, good. You're here," she said.

"You're here together?" I asked.

"I only just arrived," Agent Redmond said.

Clara gave me a nervous smile and smoothed her hair. "Quinn and I ran into each other earlier and he asked if there were any good watering holes in town. I mentioned I might be coming here tonight."

I wondered whether Clara expected us both to show up or if she'd been hedging her bets.

"Would you like a drink?" Agent Redmond asked.

"Sure." I wasn't planning on drinking when I arrived, but now I considered it a necessity. Agent Redmond and Clara? No thanks.

"She'll have the house cocktail," Clara told him.

Agent Redmond dutifully made his way to the counter.

I glanced around the busy bar. "Where's the impressive people watching?" Other than being packed, everything seemed normal.

"The deejay is on a break," Clara said. "You'll see when he comes back."

Now I was really curious. "No Sassy tonight?"

"She'll be here shortly," Clara said. "She's waiting for Tanner to get home."

"So the four of you are double dating now?" I couldn't hide my petulant tone.

"It isn't like that," Clara said. "It was all spur of the moment."

"Invite Neville along and we'll make it a triple," Agent Redmond said, returning with my drink.

"First of all, no," I said, accepting the cocktail. "Second of all, I would think you'd frown upon workplace romance. Isn't that against FBM policy?"

"Relax, Agent Fury. It's no big deal," Agent Redmond said.

Agent Redmond seemed to think an illegible signature was a big deal, so I couldn't imagine he looked the other way when it came to office romances.

"What you get up to in the privacy of your own homes is your business," Agent Redmond added.

"We don't get up to anything," I said.

"She lives in her mother's attic," Clara interjected.

Agent Redmond sucked in a breath. "Ooh, then I can see how that might be awkward."

My face grew warm. "I'm not involved with Neville outside of work. It has nothing to do with the attic. Besides, I'll have a place of my own soon enough."

"The barn," Clara said.

Agent Redmond arched an eyebrow. "You're moving from an attic to a barn?"

"It's being converted into a home," I said. "And it's going to be amazing." Once John actually finished the renovation.

"Not to be difficult," Agent Redmond, "but if you want to create distance from your family, then why not get a place completely your own?"

I folded my arms. "Look at you with the hard-hitting questions. And here I thought Clara was the rising journalist."

"It's complicated," Clara told him.

"Family always is," Agent Redmond replied. "Would you like another drink, Clara?"

58

"Yes, please," she said.

He stepped away as the music started.

"Oh, good. The deejay's back," Clara said.

"Can we talk about you and Quinn?" I asked, emphasizing the agent's first name.

She shushed me. "Not now. This is too good to miss."

Someone's best impression of Adele reached my ears. I stood on the tips of my toes for a better view. "Is that Mr. Pope from the hardware store?"

"Sure is," Clara said. "Big Adele fan, apparently. This is his third song of hers tonight."

"Wow," I said. "He really wants to set fire to the rain."

"I'd say he's adamant about it," Clara said. "It's been like this all night."

I glanced at her. "Bad singing? Isn't that standard for karaoke?"

"Not just that. I've been coming here for years and the same people always sing. Tonight, it's people who have never once set foot near the microphone."

"Like Mr. Pope?"

She nodded. "The woman before him, Kathy Daley. She's a secretary at the company Tanner works for. She's usually quiet as a mouse, but her voice sounds like a fox's mating call."

"What did she sing?"

"*Wrecking Ball* by Miley Cyrus. Did a lot of the sexy moves, too."

I cringed. "I'm sorry I missed that one."

"Why do you think I called you?"

"I guess they're drunk," I said.

"Look around," Clara said. "Everyone in here is drunk. Everyone."

I surveyed the bar. Although it was hard to tell at a glance,

I saw enough people wobbling and laughing loudly to believe her.

"What about you?" I asked. "You're holding your own."

She gave me a pointed look. "I knew Quinn was likely to show and yet I called you anyway. I'm pretty drunk."

"I think it's the fog," I said. "It's making people act out."

Agent Redmond returned with her drink. "I've always been intrigued by karaoke," he said.

"Any song in particular?" I asked.

"I quite enjoy pop music," he replied.

Okay, anyone who referred to it as 'pop music' couldn't possibly enjoy it. "Step right up. I won't report you." But I might film it on my phone and keep it for blackmail purposes.

Another song began and I recognized the 80's hit *Mickey* by Toni Basil. Well, I wish it was the Toni Basil version. In my mind, the singer was Godzilla and the song was Tokyo.

"That's Babs Foreman from the pharmacy," Clara said. "I've never seen her here before."

"Let's hope we never see her here again," I said. "At least for karaoke night."

"I'm going to add my name to the list," Agent Redmond said. "Will you sing with me, Clara?"

"Okay," she replied without hesitation. Agent Redmond threaded his way through the crowd to sign them up.

I balked. "You're going to sing?"

"Everyone else is. Why not me?" she replied.

"You won't even sing in the shower," I said to Clara. "You said you're afraid the neighbors might hear you."

"This is different," Clara said.

Was the bartender slipping something special into the alcohol? I sniffed my drink. Smelled normal to me.

"I hope he picks up a romantic duet," Clara said. "Maybe *Endless Love.*"

I gave her a strange look but said nothing. Clara and I were only just finding our footing as friends again after a years-long hiatus. I didn't want to jeopardize it with unsolicited advice.

"Yay! They're here," Clara said.

My gut twisted as Tanner and Sassafras 'Sassy' Persimmons made their way toward us. They were inarguably the most attractive couple here. She was the epitome of a blond bombshell and he had the kind of non-threatening, handsome looks that made him equally popular among men and women. No small wonder they both worked in sales now.

"What's the occasion?" Tanner asked, observing the crowd. "You'd think they were giving away free drinks."

"The karaoke is a big draw tonight," Clara said.

On cue, the next song began. *My Way* by the unfortunate singer that was not Frank Sinatra. Sassy wrinkled her nose.

"Is there an exotic bird up there?" she complained.

"Novices, apparently," I said. "Clara said people who never sing have suddenly decided tonight's their night to be a star."

"Don't they know they're terrible?" Tanner craned his neck to glimpse the singer. "And he's not even good-looking. If you're going to sound like that, you should at least be easy on the eyes."

"Pass him a note," I said. "I'm sure he'll appreciate the feedback."

Agent Redmond cut through the crowd and reached for Clara's hand. "We're up next. I paid the deejay twenty dollars to move us up the list."

Agent Redmond bribed the deejay? How drunk was he?

Someone bumped me from behind and spilled beer down my back. Hysterical laughter followed and I whipped around to confront the assailant.

"Shirley?" My grandmother's best friend was yucking it

61

up with an older man in a short-sleeved shirt and a skinny tie. They looked like they'd arrived straight from the basement of a church social.

Shirley looked down her nose at me. "Drinking is a sin, Eden Fury." She then proceeded to gulp down the rest of her beer.

"Shirley, you promised me a dance," the older man said.

She snaked an arm around his waist. "Fine, honey, but no fornication in the men's bathroom. I don't care how much you beg. Fornication is a sin, too."

"But I *like* sin," her companion replied.

She ruffled his hair. "Bernie, you're so funny." They continued past me to merge with the karaoke crowd.

Okay, *that* was weird.

"*Love Shack*," Sassy said. "I love this song."

I listened intently. The male voice sounded oddly familiar. Then I heard the female voice and I knew.

"Shock emoji," Sassy said. "That's Clara!"

I pushed my way through the onlookers to see Agent Redmond and Clara singing their hearts out. Agent Redmond was gyrating his hips and stomping his foot in time to the music while Clara shimmied. Everyone in the bar seemed to be jumping and down to the beat, even the old man in the corner with a cane.

"They're awesome," Sassy said, bopping beside me.

"They're something," I replied. I couldn't tear my gaze away. What had gotten into Agent Redmond? Was he that lovestruck that he wanted to impress Clara with his karaoke skills? But that didn't explain Clara. She avoided attention like the plague, yet here she was in the spotlight.

Clara's words echoed in my mind—*tonight, it's people who have never once set foot near the microphone*. I took a closer look at the bar patrons. It seemed like more than people who didn't typically sing. It was also people who didn't typically drink. Shirley was in the middle of the makeshift dance floor, swinging her arms in the air. Shirley once told me I was going to hell because my mother had let me taste her wine during Christmas dinner. I was only eleven at the time.

What on earth was going on?

Clara and Agent Redmond finished their song and leaped down from the stage like a pair of professional Vegas performers. Clara's cheeks were flushed with pride—or maybe it was alcohol.

Sassy managed to jump between us before I could say anything. "That was seriously great," she said.

Clara's arms were around Agent Redmond's waist. "Thanks. It was so much fun."

"Impressive performance," I said. "I didn't know you had it in you, Agent Redmond."

He seemed perfectly at ease with Clara wrapped around him like a twist tie on a bread bag.

"I need the bathroom," I said loudly.

"Congratulations," Sassy replied.

I kept my gaze on Clara. "You've had a lot to drink. I bet you need to go, too."

"Oh," Clara said, picking up on my request. "Oh, right. I do need to pee. Like Niagara Falls." She extricated herself from Agent Redmond and accompanied me to the bathroom. I dragged her into the handicapped stall and locked the door.

"What's going on with you?" I demanded.

"I felt like singing," she said.

"Not the karaoke—although that was bizarre—I mean Agent Redmond."

She smiled dreamily. "Eden, you should feel the emotions stirring inside him. He's such a good guy."

"Emotions stirring in Agent Redmond?" I found that hard to believe.

63

"I'm surprised you haven't picked up on his energy," Clara said. "He's the perfect blend of…"

I placed my hand over her mouth. "Listen to yourself. You're not making sense. Quinn Redmond is only here for less than two weeks. He's doing his job for the FBM and then he's gone."

She bit my finger and I let go with a yelp. "Who cares how long he's here for? I really like him and you know I never let myself like anybody."

"That's my point," I said. "What are you doing? This isn't like you."

Clara burped and giggled. "I told you I'm drunk. What's the big deal? Let's not count the number of times I've seen you drunk."

There would be no reasoning with her right now. "Something weird is going on."

Clara pulled down her pants and sat on the toilet. I stared in horror, not because she was peeing in front of me (that was nothing new) but because she didn't place her usual two strips of toilet paper on the seat first. Drunk or not, Clara always covered the seat with paper.

"Why are you on the toilet?" I asked.

She squinted at me. "Why do you think?"

"You didn't put paper down."

"There wasn't time. I needed to go."

Enough was enough. "I'm going to drive you home now," I said.

She finished on the toilet and pulled up her pants. "I don't want to leave. It's fun."

"Something's not right," I said. "Whatever it is, I don't want you involved in it." I unlocked the stall door and waited while she washed her hands.

"I'm not going. I want to kiss Quinn."

"Just because you want to doesn't mean you should."

She glanced at me while she dried her hands. "Why not? He's handsome. He likes me, too. What's the harm?"

"I don't know yet," I said, escorting her from the bathroom.

"Yet? What does that mean?"

I hurried through the crowd before Agent Redmond or Sassy spotted us. People were hanging all over each other like it was a high school dance. I wanted her free and clear of any other influences. We made it to the door as someone began to croon *All by Myself*. I pushed her outside and slammed the door closed behind us. It felt like a narrow escape, though I didn't really know why.

"Still foggy," Clara said, poking her finger through the thick mist.

"I'll take my time," I said.

She sighed. "I was hoping to hear Quinn say that tonight."

I grabbed her by the hand and dragged her to my car. "Night's over, Clara."

She shook off my hand. "Whoa, emotion overload."

"Sorry." I unlocked the car doors and deposited Clara inside. "We'll get your car tomorrow."

She put her feet up on the dashboard and closed her eyes. "You're not evil, Eden. I know you think I only say that because you're my best friend, but even if I didn't know you, I could tell that just by touching you." Her head lolled to the side and I could see that she was falling asleep.

"Thanks, Clara. I hope you still feel that way tomorrow."

"Why?" she murmured. "What's tomorrow?"

"When you realize that I robbed you of the chance to have sex tonight."

She made kissing noises that eventually morphed into gentle snores. I buckled her seatbelt, put on the fog lights, and headed for Clara's house.

CHAPTER SEVEN

I woke up the next morning feeling less refreshed than I would've liked. Every dream seemed to involve poker chips and karaoke. One dream even involved Agent Redmond eating poker chips out of a bag like they were potato chips. I didn't need weird dreams. Real life was strange enough at the moment.

I dressed and headed downstairs for breakfast, where I inhaled the smell of freshly baked cinnamon rolls.

"Thank you, Aunt Thora," I said. She was the most skilled in the kitchen of anyone here. Agent Redmond asked why I chose to live so close to my family—Aunt Thora's culinary skills played a major role in that decision. I hated to cook, but I liked to eat.

"You're welcome. You came home late last night." My great aunt sat at the table, squeezing a slice of lemon into her tea. Grandma sat beside her, attacking her cinnamon roll with vigor.

"It was a long day," I said. I took a small plate from the cabinet and chose the largest cinnamon roll with the most icing from the cooling rack.

66

"I heard singing from the attic," Grandma said. "I thought maybe you met someone."

"It was probably while I was dreaming," I said. I took a bite of the cinnamon roll and my body instantly relaxed. It was a slice of paradise.

"Eden would never bring someone back here," Aunt Thora said.

"True, even her mother keeps her dalliances discrete," Grandma said.

The timer beeped and Aunt Thora stood to remove a second tray from the oven. "I know people who live with their grown children, so they bring their dates to the senior center after hours. Very naughty."

"Why do you think I bring hand sanitizer whenever I go there?" Grandma said.

I grimaced at the thought. "Do you know Jaclyn Brewster?"

"I've heard her name around the senior center," Aunt Thora said. She left the tray to cool and returned to the table. "Why?"

"She runs poker games out of her house, apparently."

Aunt Thora nodded. "Yes, that's right. I don't know her personally, but everyone talks about her game nights. They're supposed to be a real hoot."

"Do you know if she's a supernatural?" I asked.

Anton zipped into the room, his hair disheveled, and snagged a cinnamon roll from the second tray. He bit right into it and yowled dramatically before filling a glass with water and gulping it down.

"You could've warned me," he said accusingly.

"They're on a baking tray on top of the oven," I said. "What do you want—a flashing neon sign? Take one from the cooling rack."

"Only fools rush in," Aunt Thora said.

Grandma looked at me. "That explains your parents' shotgun wedding."

Anton was more concerned with his breakfast than his bastard status. "I'm hungry and I need to go to work. I'm running late."

"Which kind of work?" Grandma asked.

Anton poured a cup of coffee. "Only one job cares if I'm late."

"Stop trying to stir the cauldron," I said to my grandmother. She knew perfectly well that I disapproved of my brother taking vengeance jobs on the side. He seemed to find more creative fulfillment with the ad agency, but the side jobs were paying for his home renovations.

"Who me?" Grandma asked, fluttering her eyelashes.

Anton wolfed down the roll. "Where's Mom?"

"Getting ready for yoga," Grandma said.

"Yoga?" I repeated. "Since when?"

"Since some hot guy decided to teach the class," Grandma said.

I shoved aside the images of my mother in a variety of poses designed to tempt the teacher. I felt sorry for him already.

"Jaclyn Brewster," I said, in an effort to return to our earlier conversation. "Is she a supernatural?"

"I haven't met her, so I don't know," Aunt Thora said.

"What's with the interest?" Grandma asked. "Does she owe you money?"

"No, but someone lost a lot of money in one of her poker games. I want to make sure what she's doing there is kosher."

"Now you're the fun police, too?" Anton asked.

"She's always been the chief of the fun police," Grandma said. "Who lost money?"

"None of your business," I said. I went to the counter to

retrieve a second cinnamon roll. The moment my hand touched it, the roll grew hot, melting the icing. "Hey!"

Grandma cackled. "That's what you get for telling me to mind my own business."

I snatched another roll and bit into it before she could hex it.

"Quick reflexes," Anton said with admiration.

"And yet she hates her powers," Grandma said. "If it weren't for being a fury, she wouldn't be enjoying that cinnamon roll right now."

"A small consolation," I said. "By the way, I saw Shirley last night at The Cheese Wheel."

"My Shirley?" Grandma asked.

"No, Shirley Temple. Of course your Shirley. She was drunk and dancing."

Grandma laughed. "Nice try. I think you did see Shirley Temple."

"I'm not lying. She was with some older guy named Bernie. They looked cozy."

Grandma examined me. "You're telling the truth."

"Of course I am."

"Shirley was drunk?" Aunt Thora asked in disbelief. "Did you make sure she was okay? Maybe someone spiked her drink."

"I don't think so," I said. "Everyone at The Cheese Wheel was having a grand old time. I think it's this fog making people stir crazy. They needed somewhere to go to get the kinks out."

"It does make you feel closed in," Anton agreed. "I miss the sun." He finished his roll and reached for another one.

"Are you sure you want to eat that?" my mother asked, appearing in the kitchen in her yoga pants and tank top. "Goes straight to your middle."

I was wondering whether she'd sense the carb overindulgence from her bedroom.

"I feel comfortable with my middle," Anton said and bit into the roll.

"I'm sure Verity does, too," my mother said. "Probably makes a nice pillow for her head at night."

Anton looked at the remainder of the roll before setting it on the counter. "I'll see everyone for dinner. I need to go."

I scooped up his discarded roll and ate it.

"It's one thing to rescue a hellhound, Eden," my mother said. "It's another thing to rescue a baked good. You're only hurting yourself."

"Whatever," I said, my mouth full of cinnamon roll. Now I wanted a latte to wash it down. "I'm heading out for training as soon as I brush my teeth. See you later."

"I'd walk if I were you," my mother called after me. "Burn off those rolls."

"And the baked good, too!" Grandma added.

I ignored them both and went to the bathroom before leaving the house.

Thanks to the thickening fog, I drove ten miles an hour all the way to my office. Agent Redmond was already inside with Neville. They stood across from each other at the back table discussing one of Neville's inventions.

"Good morning, Agent Redmond," I said. "Neville."

"Good morning," Agent Redmond said. He glanced down at my T-shirt that read *Sorry I'm Late But I Didn't Want To Come*. "Sort of like wearing your heart on your sleeve, isn't it?"

"My family doesn't do subtle." I noticed a bright pink box on the table from Holes, the donut shop next door. "Too bad I already ate."

"No worries," Neville said. "They're all gone."

My eyes popped. "You ate them all?"

"Agent Redmond helped."

I blinked. "You helped? But you don't like carbs."

"Normally, I avoid them, but Neville mentioned how delicious they are and I couldn't resist," he said. "I've discovered I'm a fan of the custard cream."

"Feeling a bit rough today?" I asked.

His expression gave nothing away. "I feel fine, thank you."

"I ran into Agent Redmond at the bar last night," I said.

Neville seemed surprised. "I suppose there isn't much else to do in the evenings with this weather."

"Agent Redmond seemed to find plenty to keep him occupied," I said. "It was karaoke night."

Agent Redmond flinched.

"Ooh, lovely," Neville said. "I enjoy a good rendition of *Danny Boy* every now and again."

"He opted for something more contemporary," I said. "A duet with Clara."

"We should get on with our training," Agent Redmond said quickly. "I thought we'd run through standard operating procedures today."

"Like what?" I asked. I thought we'd exhausted every rule and regulation in the book by now.

"Like what you do when you detect a supernatural interference in town," he replied.

"I've done that twice already," I said.

"She has," Neville interjected. "Most impressive, too. I'm not sure that Paul Pidcock would've been as competent."

Agent Redmond ignored Neville. "I'm sure you think our procedures are unnecessary bureaucracy, but I assure you..."

"I don't think that," I said. "I followed FBI rules without incident." Until the incident with Fergus, of course, but I'd had no intention of breaking any rules.

"Good. Glad to hear it," Agent Redmond said. "Then this should be a cake walk for you."

71

"Mmm. Cake walk," I said.

Agent Redmond regarded me. "You do realize it's just an expression."

"One can hope."

"Tell me, Agent Fury, what's the first thing you do when you realize there's a supernatural force at work?"

"Freak out," I said.

A look of annoyance flashed across his angular features. "Then what?"

"I try to determine whether it crosses an acceptable line," I said. "Is the force disruptive to the natural order? If so, then I know I have to act."

"And how do you make that determination?" Agent Redmond asked.

"A lucky guess?" I offered weakly.

"The rules are written for you, Agent Fury. There's no need to guess. Did you guess as an agent for the FBI or did you follow protocol?"

"I followed protocol."

"Exactly, so why not now?" Agent Redmond asked.

I fell back against my chair and spun around. "Can I have fun Agent Redmond back? This guy is stifling."

"Agent Fury, I'm surprised by your attitude. Your file suggests that you were an upstanding FBI agent who thrived under deadlines and clearly defined parameters."

I kicked out my foot to stop my chair from spinning. "That's true. That does describe me."

"Then how do you explain your resistance now?"

I thought for a moment. "I guess I've just hit my limit. I've been forced back to my hometown. Forced into a job I didn't want. Maybe I'm starting my rebellious stage."

"Shouldn't you have started that about ten years ago?" Agent Redmond asked.

I turned on my computer. "What are your intentions with Clara?"

"He has intentions with Clara?" Neville asked.

"That's what I'm trying to find out," I said.

Agent Redmond pointed a slender finger at me. "Don't try to deflect, Agent Fury. How do you handle a potential supernatural interference?"

I leaned my head against the back of the chair and swiveled back and forth. "I'll do better than tell you. I'll show you."

"Show me how?"

"I need to pay a visit to someone who may or may not be a supernatural," I said. "If she is a supernatural, then there's a chance she's up to something."

"Sounds promising," Agent Redmond said.

I frowned at him. "I hope not. I don't want there to be any interference."

He dragged a hand through his hair. "Yes, of course. You know what I mean."

I vaulted from my chair. "I'm going to see a woman named Jaclyn Brewster."

"And what's her alleged crime?" Agent Redmond asked.

"I don't know yet."

"What kind of supernatural is she?"

"I don't know yet."

He cocked his head. "What do you know, Agent Fury?"

"That she runs poker games for senior citizens out of her house and one of them lost his retirement savings."

Agent Redmond scratched his head. "That...doesn't sound supernatural."

I grabbed my handbag from the desk and headed for the door. "I guess I'll let you know when I figure it out."

CHAPTER EIGHT

I DIDN'T GO straight to Jaclyn Brewster's house. First, I went to perform my daily check on the portal. No changes there.

On the walk back to my car, I noticed Chief Fox's car move slowly toward me and waved. He came to a stop and rolled down the window.

"What are you doing out here?" he asked. "Haven't you seen the advisory to stay indoors?"

"I can't stay inside all day," I said. "I get itchy."

"Sounds more like a skin condition," he said. "At least you've got your sun lamp." Chief Fox had given me a sun lamp for my office as a thank you for helping him solve Chief O'Neill's murder. Of course, he didn't know a fear demon was the real culprit.

"Any idea when this fog will pass?" I asked.

"Weather reports vary," he said. "I wish I had a direct line to Mother Nature, but I don't."

"I bet you never had fog like this in Iowa," I said. Chief Fox was born and raised in Des Moines. I'd tried to learn more about Iowa so I had talking points, but I seemed to lose brain cells in his presence.

74

"Definitely not," he said. "I don't think anyone's equipped for a siege like this."

"I guess you're still patrolling overtime," I said. "Let me know if you'd like more help with that."

He brightened. "Any help you want to give would be great. Is your FBI friend still in town? We could use him, too."

"He is, but he's otherwise engaged," I said.

"Well, I've requested help from neighboring counties," Chief Fox said. "The fog seems to be intent on hanging around Chipping Cheddar, so at least no one else is suffering."

I smiled. "It *is* a nice town."

"I've definitely warmed to it." He smiled back and an awkward silence followed. We'd already discussed the weather. Everything else I wanted to say either involved too much information, a sexual overture, or an inappropriate remark about the dimple in his chin.

Get it together, Eden.

"I'm thinking about instituting a curfew until the fog lifts," Chief Fox said.

"That's a good idea," I said. "It might cut down on the petty crime."

"That's the hope." Another car pulled behind the chief and he started the engine. "I should get back to patrolling."

"Yeah, I have work to do, too," I said. "See you around."

He gave me another fleeting look before rolling up his window and driving away. He was probably disappointed that Agent Redmond couldn't help. If the chief was willing to pull in cops from neighboring counties, he must really feel out of his depth right now.

I decided to get my visit to Jaclyn Brewster out of the way so that I could report back to Agent Redmond and give him the protocol details he wanted. I drove to one of the nicer neighborhoods in town off Mozzarella Road. Jaclyn lived in a stucco house that would've looked more at home in Arizona than Maryland.

A statuesque woman answered the door wearing a purple floor-length dress and I immediately heard a soft hiss emanate from beneath her floral headscarf.

"You're a Gorgon," I said. Well, if nothing else, I established that she was in fact, a supernatural.

Her smile was tight. "I have a house full of humans downstairs. You should be a little more careful, Miss…"

"Agent Eden Fury." I displayed my badge.

Her eyes widened almost imperceptibly. "I see. Do come in out of this wretched fog."

The foyer was elegantly appointed with a simple crystal chandelier above and an antique secretary against the wall. A multi-colored Shiraz rug covered the wooden floor. The interior didn't match the exterior at all.

"Are the humans downstairs from the senior center?" I asked.

She started. "As a matter of fact, they are."

"I understand you host a lot of game nights for them," I said.

She pressed her fingertips together. "I do. It's my form of community service. It's so much more pleasant to enjoy a game in the comfort of someone's home than a stuffy municipal building."

"Do you consider it community service to swindle an old man out of his retirement savings?" Oops. I didn't intend to go there so quickly.

Her hands dropped to her sides. "You're referring to Simon Travers, I take it?"

"Are there others?"

Her snakes hissed loudly, as though insulted on her

behalf. "Of course not. Poker doesn't typically get out of control like that. The whole evening was unusual."

"Why did you let it get out of hand?"

"The game seemed to take on a life of its own," Jaclyn said. "Everyone's bets became increasingly outrageous. One of the men even offered his wife when he ran out of chips."

"I assume he was joking."

Jaclyn gave me a pointed look. "I'm quite certain he wasn't."

"If it went overboard, why not put a stop to it? Cancel the game?"

Jaclyn adjusted the hem of her headscarf when one of the snake's tails slipped out, not that a human would have seen it. The snakes were only visible to supernaturals and humans with the Sight.

"To be honest, I didn't even grasp the enormity of the situation until the next day when I remembered the look on Simon's face. It was gut-wrenching."

"But not so gut-wrenching that you drove over there and gave him his money back," I said. "Do you know his wife got arrested for beating him? She was so distraught over the loss of the money, that she lost her temper."

"That's a shame," Jaclyn said, "but I've learned humans can behave strangely when money's involved."

A loud whoop came from downstairs.

Jaclyn laughed lightly. "Today's game also seems to be getting out of hand."

"No one's giving up their retirement accounts, I hope."

"No, it isn't their retirement accounts they're giving up."

Her Mona Lisa smile set my radar pinging. "What's going on down there?"

Clapping thundered below my feet.

"Another poker game," Jaclyn said vaguely.

"Sounds fun," I said, eyeing her suspiciously. "Maybe I should join in."

"I don't think this particular game will appeal to you."

"I think I'll be the judge of that," I said.

Jaclyn hesitated a brief moment before gesturing for me to follow her. We descended a staircase at the end of the hallway that emptied into a finished basement.

A pool table and a bar were at one end of the huge room and a large round table was at the other. A bartender in a tuxedo poured drinks behind the bar.

"Would you like a drink?" Jaclyn asked. "Alfredo makes a mean Manhattan."

I was too stunned to answer. My gaze had drifted to the poker game at the other end of the room where seven senior citizens sat around the table.

Naked.

Or mostly naked.

"Welcome," a bald man called. He wore tube socks and white boxers with red hearts. That was it.

"Ooh, fresh fish," a woman said. "Reel her in, Jaclyn."

Jaclyn nudged me toward the table.

"No way," a white-haired woman said. "Her skin is too youthful and glowing. No age spots means no seat at the table." Only a string of pearls and granny panties covered her.

"There's no age spot rule, Helen. Stop trying to create one. Sit down and join us," a man said. He wore a knit cap, a green polka dot tie, and nothing else. Not a stitch of clothing.

"She can't join the game now, Bob," the woman beside him said. "We're almost through this round. Besides, we all know Myrna is going to win anyway."

"That's because she cheats," another woman said, with a spiteful glance in the direction of a frosty blonde I assumed was the aforementioned Myrna.

"I'll cut you off at the knees, Janice," Myrna said, pointing a menacing finger at the silver-haired woman. Myrna seemed to be wearing the most articles of clothing, including a fedora and a feather boa.

"You'll have to make it through her boobs to get to them," Bob said. "They may be low, but they're surprisingly dense."

Myrna smacked Bob's arm. "Why do you know so much about her boob density?"

He held out a helpless hand. "This is our fourth round. She hasn't won them all."

My hand flew to cover my eyes. I'd seen enough.

"Ladies and gentlemen, if I could please ask that you put your clothes back on," I said. "This game is officially over."

Groans of protest followed my announcement.

"Youth is wasted on the young," someone grumbled.

"We have to finish the game," Myrna insisted. "I'm finally winning."

"Finish it without the stripping then," I said. "And get dressed."

Players began to collect items of clothing from the floor around them.

"Ouch, I pulled a muscle in my back," Bob said as he leaned down to get his clothes.

"The one time I decide to get naked and this happens," Janice complained.

"At least I spotted that discolored freckle on your chest," Helen said. "Now you can make an appointment with the dermatologist and get it checked out."

"I didn't come here for an exam," Janice said. "I came here to get lucky."

Sweet Hecate. I really hoped she was talking about the poker game.

"You haven't gotten lucky since the bicentennial," Myrna snapped.

Janice glared at her. "At least I didn't have to call timeout during pickleball due to excessive hot flashes."

Myrna shot to her feet. "They were distracting!"

Oh boy.

Jaclyn smirked and tried to hand me a drink, but I waved it away. "Aren't you glad you insisted on coming down here?" she asked.

I dragged her to the far corner of the room. "No more of this. Do you understand?"

"Why not? I'm not breaking any rules," she said.

I glanced back at the table. "You're not using any Gorgon mojo on them?"

"What mojo would that be?" Jaclyn asked. "I have snakes for hair, not that humans can see them. I can turn people to stone if I choose to use my powers, but I know that's a one-way ticket back to Otherworld. I'm not that stupid. I like it here."

"So these people are always half naked in your basement?" I asked.

Jaclyn bit her lip. "Well, not really. Like I mentioned, things have been a little out of control lately. This is the first time anyone thought strip poker was a good idea."

"Maybe stop plying them with alcohol and they'll keep their clothes on," I said.

"I don't think it took very much alcohol to get to this point."

I was relieved to see most of the players had put their clothes back on. "I'll tell you what, Jaclyn. You refund Simon Travers' money and I won't report you to the FBM."

"Report me for what? I haven't done anything wrong."

"Any kind of supernatural interference in human life can be construed as a violation, depending on the outcome," I said. "Simon Travers and his wife have no money left. That's a pretty big interference by a supernatural, whether you used powers or not." No idea whether that argument would hold up, but Uncle Moyer would've been proud of me.

She pressed her hand against her chest. "I can't return money. It will set a bad precedent."

"No one has to know," I said.

"I didn't force him to bet like a crazy person. That was his choice."

I pointed to the poker table. "Crazy seems to happen down here. Unless you want me to take a greater interest in your activities, you'll cooperate."

Jaclyn folded her arms and huffed. "The house always wins, Agent Fury. That's the way it works."

"Refund his money tomorrow," I said. "Or I'll be back with that one-way ticket you mentioned."

The snakes hissed and I hissed back.

Her dark eyes blazed with indignation. "Fine. Consider it done."

CHAPTER NINE

"EDEN, COME DOWN," my mother called. "Dinner's almost ready."

Alice and I were on the mattress in front of the television, watching *Dirty Dancing*. At first, she'd been shocked by the style of dancing, much like Baby Houseman, but she seemed to come around.

"In a minute," I yelled.

Alice pointed to the remote. "You can pause it if you want."

"That's okay. I've seen it fifty times." I stood and stretched. It had been another long day and my stomach was ready for a home-cooked meal.

"You should brush your hair before you go down," Alice said.

I rolled my eyes. "Not you, too."

"Of course not, dear. I think your hair looks fine. Consider it preemptive."

"It won't matter," I said. "My mother will latch on to something else if the hair looks good. One time she

82

commented on the shape of my kneecaps, as though I have any control over those."

Alice clucked her tongue. "It isn't easy, is it?"

"Nope." I tugged a lightweight hoodie over my head and descended the stairs.

I heard the sizzle of a roasting pan before the smell of chicken wafted over to greet me.

"I thought you might be in a coma," my mother said. "I was about to send Anton to wake you." She dumped carrots from the pot into a serving bowl.

"Agent Redmond kept me busy today," I said. After I returned to the office from Jaclyn Brewster's, Agent Redmond made me compile a list of all the minor spells my family had taught me over the years. Charming locks. Transformation hexes. The whole endeavor gave me a headache just thinking about it.

"Speaking of the handsome fae, I took the liberty of inviting him to dinner," my mother said.

I started to cough. "You what? Where did you even see him?"

"I ran into him in town while you were in your coma," she said.

I cast a suspicious glance at her. "Where?"

My mother smiled and fluffed her hair. "We needed milk."

"And you ran into Agent Redmond in the convenience store?" A likely story.

"No, sweetheart. Don't be silly. I saw him in his B&B."

I smacked my forehead. "You went to my training instructor's B&B? Are you insane?"

Grandma held up a finger. "I can vouch for that."

"The B&B was on the way," my mother said airily.

"On the way to the outskirts of town," I shot back. "You had no right to do that."

My mother smacked her hands on the counter. "I had

every right. Agent Redmond is a federal agent. We need to treat him with respect."

"Since when?" I asked. "You don't treat me with respect."

"That's different," my mother said. "I gave birth you. Anything that comes out of your own nether regions is another matter entirely."

I pressed my lips together. "Do me a favor. Don't mention your nether regions at the dinner table."

"Who knows?" Grandma piped up. "If he's good-looking enough, she might show them after dinner."

I groaned. "Please don't hit on him, Mom. It's embarrassing."

"If you're interested, then I'll back off," my mother said. "My future grandchildren are more important than a tryst."

"What's a tryst?" Olivia asked from her place at the table.

Verity glared at my mother. "She said treat, honey."

My niece's eyes rounded. "Ooh, I like treats."

A smirk shaped my mother's lips. "So do I."

Charlemagne slithered across the floor, chasing a tennis ball. My grandmother's black cat jumped down from the island and knocked the ball out of the python's path. Charlemagne hissed and the black cat arched her back and hissed in response.

"It's adorable how they play together," Aunt Thora remarked.

The doorbell rang and Princess Buttercup galloped down the hall, eager to be the first one to greet—or eat our guest. It was always a risk whether she'd like the visitor. Charlemagne, on the other hand, didn't care who it was, as long as the opportunity to have his body scratched presented itself.

"Please be on your best behavior, everyone," I said.

"Define 'best,'" my mother said.

I moaned and followed the hellhound to the door. The last thing I needed was to have my trainer burned to a crisp by my dog's fiery saliva. One shake of the hound's head in close proximity to a flammable object and we risked a towering inferno.

I bumped Princess Buttercup aside with my hip and opened the door. "Welcome to chaos, Agent Redmond."

The fae stood on the front porch in a crisp navy blue suit. "It isn't often I get invited to dinner by the family of my trainee."

"You might wish that was still the case." I stepped side. "Enter at your own risk." Although I tried to remain cool and collected, my insides were churning. What if my family did or said something that piqued Agent Redmond's professional interest? He wasn't exactly laidback. If he caught Grandma with black magic paraphernalia, he wouldn't look the other way. He seemed like the kind of agent that slept with handcuffs on his bedside table, and not for any enjoyable reason.

Agent Redmond offered a relaxing smile. "I appreciate the overture."

"And Clara was busy?"

He wore a vague smile. "She's tailing one of the police officers from another county this evening while he patrols Chipping Cheddar. I told her to call if she stumbles upon anything dangerous."

Princess Buttercup sniffed his shoes. "May I present Her Royal Highness, Princess Buttercup," I said.

"Would she object if I pet her?" Agent Redmond asked.

"Give it a try. The most you'll lose is a hand," I said. He jerked toward me and I laughed. "The fact that she's checking our your shoes and not spewing fire is a good sign."

Agent Redmond gave a shaky laugh and reached down to stroke the hellhound's head. "Wherever did you find such a creature?"

"I rescued her from the bowels of the underworld," I said.

"Well, technically it was the entrance where someone had abandoned her."

Agent Redmond crouched down to get closer to her. "You are a beauty, aren't you?" He glanced up at me. "You realize her presence here is against regulations?"

"What do you mean?"

He returned to a standing position. "She's highly dangerous, to supernaturals as well as humans."

I pointed to Princess Buttercup, who was now on her back with her legs in the air, practically begging for a belly rub. "Does that look like a dangerous hellhound?"

Agent Redmond smiled at the sight. "I understand, Agent Fury. At the very least, you need to apply for a license for her. She can't be here if she's not on the books."

Silently, I cursed my mother for inviting Agent Redmond here. "Won't they refuse me a license on the grounds that it's against regulations?"

He looked at me with a serious expression. "I suspect they will. As I said, she's too dangerous."

"My family's more dangerous than she'll ever be," I snapped, and immediately regretted it. Great, now he'd be suspicious of my family from the start.

Agent Redmond chuckled. "Everyone worries about the impression their family gives. Even I was afraid to bring friends around when I was younger."

"What did you worry about—that your mother would knit too many hats in one sitting?" I pictured the Redmond family holding hands and singing around a crackling fire. They were basically the fae version of the Whos from Whoville.

"My point is that we all think we have the most embarrassing family," he said. "I'm sure yours is no worse than anyone else's."

Alice's head emerged from the wall. "I don't normally join

you for dinner, but I think this will be more interesting than the television."

I narrowed my eyes at her before turning to lead Agent Redmond into the kitchen. My family practically pounced as we rounded the corner.

"Come in, come in," my mother said, in her annoying singsong voice that she usually reserved for politicians and children she intended to lure into her gingerbread house.

"What a beautiful home you have, Mrs. Fury," Agent Redmond said.

She batted her eyelashes in a way that made me want to puke. "Please. Call me Beatrice."

He surveyed the comfy interior. "My mother always said you can tell a lot about the owners by the energy of their house."

My mother gave him a flirtatious smile. "Your mother sounds like a very wise woman. She's fae, I take it?"

Agent Redmond nodded. "We're one hundred percent fae in my family."

"I find that fascinating in this day and age. Come and meet everyone." My mother linked her arm through his and guided him to the dining table.

"This is Agent Quinn Redmond," I said, jumping in before my mother could introduce him as something inappropriate like 'my future son-in-law' or 'my next boyfriend.'

"Nice to meet you," Verity said. "How are you finding Chipping Cheddar?"

I was relieved that my sister-in-law waded in first. She was, by far, the most reasonable and well-mannered of the assembled family members. Aunt Thora was a close second, but she tended to stay quiet in a group or when strangers were within earshot.

My mother placed Agent Redmond across from me and next to her at the table. I made a valiant effort to keep the conversation light during the meal, avoiding any topic that could set off a firestorm among the witches or demons at the table.

"What's the consensus so far, Agent Redmond?" Grandma asked. "Is my granddaughter cut out for Pidcock's post?"

"Well, I didn't know Paul Pidcock," he replied, "but Agent Fury seems to have things well in hand from what I can see. It's no surprise that she's an ENTJ."

Grandma leaned forward. "A what now?"

"Her personality test," Agent Redmond said. "Her results indicate that she's an ENTJ, also known as the Commander."

My grandma barked a short laugh. "There's only one commander in this house, Agent Redmond, and that's me."

"These tests are fairly accurate," Agent Redmond said.

"I'll be the judge of that." Grandma scraped back her chair. "Where's this test so I can take it?"

"You can take it online," Anton said. "We've taken it at work."

I shot my brother a baleful look. "Don't encourage her."

"What are you?" Verity asked her husband.

"ESFP," Anton said. "The Entertainer."

Grandma made a noise at the back of her throat.

"Well, you are entertaining," my mother said. "Even as a little boy."

Grandma disappeared into the office where the computer was located with my mother and I hot on her heels.

"I should really go first," my mother said, scooting Grandma out of the way.

"Why? I was born first," Grandma replied.

My mother pulled up the website before my grandmother could object. "I need privacy or it will skew the results."

Grandma rolled her eyes. "You don't even need privacy in the bathroom. If you could wrangle an audience, you'd squeeze them into the bathtub."

"Let's go, Grandma," I said. "Your turn will come."

We vacated the office and my mother emerged a few minutes later. "I'm an ENFJ," she announced. "I'm charismatic and inspire others."

"How many times did you have to take it to get that result?" Grandma asked.

Verity laughed. "That's like you on Pottermore," she said to Anton.

"What? I'm a Gryffindor," Anton said with a look of complete innocence.

"Sure. After three test scores telling you you're a Hufflepuff," Verity replied.

Anton's cheeks reddened. "The questions were confusing!"

"My turn," Grandma said, and left the table.

We finished every scrap of food on the table, which wasn't difficult when Aunt Thora's cooking was involved. Ryan had dumped all his vegetables into the gravy boat and my mother simply slid the boat in front of him and handed him a spoon. I could tell Verity was unhappy, but didn't want to argue in front of our guest.

"Results are in," Grandma said, reappearing in the kitchen. "I'm an ENTJ, just as I suspected."

I ran into the office to check the results on the screen. "This can't be right."

Grandma smiled. "Tests don't lie. Your agent friend said so." She seemed far too pleased by this turn of events.

"We're not the same," I said.

"Sure we are," Grandma replied. "Says so right there." She tapped the screen.

"Our personalities are completely different," I said. I heard the shrill sound of my voice, but I had no control over it. "You spelled the test results, didn't you?"

"I didn't. I took them fair and square."

"You don't do anything fair and square. You even cheat at Go Fish with Olivia."

Grandma's eyes narrowed dangerously. "Watch your tongue with me, young lady, or you may find it missing in the morning. I don't care what your badge says."

"And then what? You'll add it to your burnbook?" I taunted.

Grandma continued to stare at me, daring me to press the issue. "I don't know what you're talking about."

With all the distractions lately, I'd forgotten to follow up with Neville about the locator spell. I ducked into the bathroom and whipped out my phone to dial his number.

He answered on the first ring. "Yes, Agent Fury?"

"Any luck with that locator spell I asked you to do?"

"Ah, yes. I haven't wanted to mention it in front of Agent Redmond. I'm afraid not. I believe her hair is charmed."

"What do you mean?"

"I believe she charms her hair to prevent it from being used as part of a spell such as this one."

Of course she did. "Thanks, Neville."

I marched back into the office where Grandma remained seated in front of the computer. "Do you seriously charm your hair?"

She smirked. "It only took you how many years to figure that one out, Special Agent?"

"I'm not a Special Agent," I said.

"You don't have to tell me."

I wanted to throttle my grandmother, which wasn't a particularly novel feeling but still.

I folded my arms. "I'm going to find that burnbook with or without your hair."

"In front of your training instructor?" Grandma asked. "Would you really do that to your elderly grandmother? I'm your flesh and blood."

90

"Worth it." I spun on my heel and returned to the kitchen, where Agent Redmond appeared to be dodging my mother's advances by the refrigerator. Good grief. Was nothing sacred in this house?

I zeroed in on Aunt Thora seated at the table between Anton and Verity. She looked so peaceful that I hated to ruin her evening, but she was the weak link in the current standoff with my grandmother.

I slid into the chair across from her and smiled.

"Uh oh," Anton said. "I recognize that face. You look like Mom."

I ignored him. "Aunt Thora, I require your assistance."

My aunt's throat tightened. "Of course, dear. How can I help?"

"The burnbook," I said quietly, so that Agent Redmond didn't overhear me. "Where is it?"

Fear rippled across her aging features and I felt a stab of guilt for dragging her into this. It was only temporary, though.

"I don't know anything about a burnbook," she replied.

"That's not true," Verity said. "I remember that night you got drunk on limoncello and told me all about it. You said there were several pages dedicated to me in there."

Aunt Thora's face turned a deep shade of crimson. "That was the limoncello talking."

"Was it?" I drummed my fingers on the table. "I believe we have some in the pantry."

Aunt Thora eyed me carefully. "You know I can't tell you."

I leaned across the table. "If you don't tell me right now, you might find yourself with a perpetual wedgie this week."

Her eyes rounded. "You wouldn't."

"Why not? One of you did that to me." Junior year in high school. The day of final exams. I never found out which of the three it was. I only knew that I was a laughingstock because every time I liberated the fabric from my butt crack, it got caught all over again. I was so distracted that I nearly gave up on my exams. I knew I couldn't let them win, though, so I persevered.

"It wasn't me," Aunt Thora said.

I steepled my fingers. "Tell me where the burnbook is and I won't retaliate." Over Aunt Thora's head, I saw my mother attempt to give Agent Redmond a shoulder rub. I was going to have to abandon this effort in a moment if I didn't—

"In the garden," Aunt Thora said in a harsh whisper. "She keeps it buried in the garden, near the gnome."

"Nice job, sis," Anton said appreciatively. "Keep up the bad cop. It's working for you."

I pushed back my chair. "Thank you, Aunt Thora."

"Please don't tell them it was me," she whispered.

I pretended to turn the imaginary lock on my lips, not that Grandma wouldn't be able to figure out what happened. The witch was no dummy.

I waltzed over to my mother and Agent Redmond.

"Everything okay over here?" I asked.

"Terrific." Agent Redmond took a few hurried steps toward me. "It's a shame Clara couldn't join us this evening."

"I try not to subject her to my family any more than necessary," I said. "I'll be right back. I need to take Princess Buttercup outside."

"I'll come with you," the agent said quickly. The poor guy was desperate to escape my mother. Not that I blamed him.

Honestly, I couldn't think of a good reason to say no. I whistled for the hellhound and she came running. "I'm taking Agent Redmond to see the barn," I lied.

My mother gave him a demure smile. "Hurry back now. I want to hear the rest of that story about the troll."

Agent Redmond followed us out the back door. I retrieved a shovel from the shed on my way to the gnome.

"Where's the barn?" Agent Redmond asked.

I waved a hand in the opposite direction. "Over there. You can't see it through the fog. It'll be my home soon." Not soon enough.

"Then why are we going this way?" he asked.

"So Princess Buttercup can stretch her legs," I said. "Why don't you throw a stick for her to fetch? She loves that."

Agent Redmond cast a sidelong glance at the hellhound. "I suppose I could do that."

"Have you ever had a pet, Agent Redmond?"

"No, my parents didn't want one. They didn't like mess."

"I'm starting to understand you better."

I waited for Agent Redmond to disappear in the dense fog and then made a beeline for the gnome. I knew this yard like the back of my hand, fog or no fog. I wasted no time shoveling away the dirt until I hit payday.

The moment the shovel hit something solid, I tossed it aside to peer into the hole.

And there it was.

The burnbook.

I reached down to remove it from the hole, the anticipation of victory rippling through my body. The moment the book left its burial place, however, it began to disintegrate.

"A booby trap? No!"

I tried to drop it back into the hole but to no avail. My grandmother had undoubtedly warded its hiding place so that the burnbook self-destructed if it were removed by someone other than her. I should've known better.

I kneeled in front of the hole, trying not to lose my temper.

"Agent Fury?"

I hopped to my feet and faced Agent Redmond. "Sorry about that. I remembered something I had to do."

He frowned. "You had to dig a hole?"

"To bury the gnome," I said. "It's a game I play with Princess Buttercup. She loves it. I bury the gnome and she digs it up." I made a show of tossing the gnome into the hole and filling in the dirt with the shovel.

On cue, Princess Buttercup came to sniff the overturned dirt.

"I should probably get going," Agent Redmond said. "But thank you for a lovely evening."

"I appreciate you putting up with us."

He looked uneasily at the house. "I should probably go and pay my respects."

"I won't blame you if you sneak around the side of the house."

He seemed to consider it. "It isn't gentlemanly. I'll do my duty as a guest in your home."

"Suit yourself."

When we reentered the house, Grandma was in the kitchen, stone-faced. I could tell that she knew what had happened. She watched in silence as Agent Redmond thanked everyone and said goodnight. I walked him to the door and then tried to slip away into the attic unseen. No such luck. Grandma stood at the bottom of the stairs, waiting for me.

"It's not my fault you warded it to self-destruct," I said.

Grandma did the worst thing she could possibly do.

She said nothing.

"You should've given it to me like I asked."

"It wasn't yours to take," she said simply.

We stared at each other for a moment as she took the measure of me. Younger Eden would've apologized and possibly begged for mercy. This Eden decided to do no such thing.

"That book was a physical representation of your character," I said. "If you were so concerned with its contents that you'd rather destroy it than let anyone see it, then maybe you should think about that."

"That book was none of your business, Eden Fury," she said, her tone even. "You should have left well enough alone." Then she turned and walked away.

I swallowed hard before dragging myself up to the attic. I knew there would be hell to pay—I just had no clue when I'd be paying it.

CHAPTER TEN

THE SHRILL SOUND of my phone jolted me awake. I sat bolt upright and scrambled to answer it.

"Hello?"

"Eden?" Aunt Thora's voice was shaky.

"I really need a ringtone for you," I said.

"Can you come?"

"Come where? What's wrong?"

"I'm at the lighthouse. I came to have breakfast with Ted. With all this fog, he hasn't wanted to leave, so I said I'd keep him company." Aunt Thora had been involved with Ted O'Neill, the former chief's brother, before she got married, but my family had advised against a relationship with a human. Now that she was older, my great-aunt seemed more willing to do as she pleased.

My head was too groggy to think straight. "Did a ship crash?"

"No, but someone died. We've called the police, but I'd feel better if you were here."

"You think it's supernatural related?"

"I honestly don't know," she said. "This fog is getting

96

increasingly unsettling, though. There's something about it that gives me the creeps."

If the fog was giving Aunt Thora the creeps, that was saying something. This was a woman who'd been married to a demon for decades, after all.

"I'll be there as quickly as I can," I said, and hung up.

I threw on the same clothes from yesterday that were still in a pile on the floor. Then I hurried downstairs and grabbed my car keys off the kitchen counter.

"Where do you think you're going?" Grandma asked. She stood at the island with a butcher knife in her hand. It was unclear what she was doing because there was no food on the island.

I took a step backward. I knew she was still angry about the burnbook. "Aunt Thora called. There's been an incident and she wants me there."

"Are you Batman now? Something happens and you automatically get a signal?"

"She's not sure what happened, so she thought it best if I came to the scene," I said.

"Your aunt is a worrywart," Grandma said. She waved the knife around in a way that made me glad I wasn't standing closer to her.

"Regardless, she asked me to come, so I am."

"Doing as you're told," Grandma said. "How novel."

I turned and rolled my eyes so she couldn't see me. When I was thirteen, I rolled my eyes at something she said and woke up blind the next day. She refused to reinstate my vision until I apologized. I had a math test, so I had no choice but to capitulate. You would think her harsh punishment would have stopped me from rolling my eyes, but it didn't.

I hurried from the house, my heart hammering in my chest. Who died and how did Aunt Thora witness it?

It took me double the usual time to drive to the lighthouse because of the fog. I could hardly see a foot in front of the car, so I kept a slow and steady pace. By the time I arrived, the chief's car was already there.

I took the long and winding staircase to the top, where Chief Fox was talking to Ted and Aunt Thora. The back view of the chief was every bit as good as the front and I was almost disappointed when he turned to look at me.

"What happened?" I asked.

"You could at least pretend to be winded," Aunt Thora said.

"I'm twenty-six and in shape," I said. "Why would I pretend otherwise?"

"For the sake of my ego, of course," she replied.

Chief Fox's grim expression remained intact. "Someone took a shortcut from the top of the lighthouse to the ground."

I gasped. "How awful."

"His body's been taken away, but I wanted to speak with Mr. O'Neill and your aunt about what they witnessed."

"Have you identified him?" I asked.

"I was just getting to that," Chief Fox said. "He had his wallet on him. Does the name Manfred Rice ring a bell to anyone?"

"Not me," I said.

Ted and Aunt Thora shook their heads in unison.

"I think he might be one of Gary Rice's boys," Ted said. "The Rices were one of the town's founding families."

"Gary's been dead for at least ten years," Aunt Thora added. "I remember because he had a heart attack at the senior center during a particularly intense game of pickleball."

"At my age, I think an intense game of pickleball would give me a heart attack, too," Ted said.

"We have a call into Manfred's wife," Chief Fox said. "Can

you tell me everything you saw? Was he alone? Did you hear him say anything?"

"It's pretty straightforward," Ted said. "He climbed up and jumped. There was no one with him."

"How can you be sure?" Chief Fox asked.

"Thora and I were at the window," he replied. "We thought we spotted a pod of dolphins in the bay, but it was hard to tell because of the fog." He looked at Aunt Thora for confirmation and she nodded.

"Everything blends together out there," Aunt Thora added. "I noticed the man out of the corner of my eye and told Ted that someone was scaling the side of the lighthouse."

"How is that possible?" Chief Fox asked.

"Oh, he wouldn't be the first to climb it," Ted said. "It's sort of a like a badge of honor in this town to say you've done it."

"But they don't usually rely on gravity to get back down again," Aunt Thora said.

"The fella didn't waste any time," Ted said. "I barely had a chance to react to what Thora said before he plunged to the ground."

"Then he could've fallen rather than jumped," Chief Fox said. "Maybe his foot slipped."

"Either way, it doesn't sound like a homicide," I said.

"No, it doesn't," Chief Fox agreed. "Thanks for your help. If you wouldn't mind giving official witness statements down at the station, that would be great."

"Now?" Ted asked. "I can't abandon my post, Chief."

"No, of course not, especially with this fog," the chief replied. "As soon as you can, though."

As the chief spoke, I became acutely aware of how close I was standing to him. His familiar scent of fresh pine and sea salt filled my nostrils and I resisted the urge to brush my body against his. The back of my neck grew hot at the thought and I tried to redirect my focus. A man just fell to his death and all I wanted to do was run my fingers through the chief's hair. I was turning into a monster faster than I expected.

"No dog again today, huh?" I blurted. It was the first thought that came to mind, but it did the trick. My body cooled and my thoughts calmed. Crisis averted.

"No," Chief Fox said, "but there's a pug named Charlie that was brought into the shelter this week. I'd love to get him out on patrol once the fog is gone."

"You should think about a companion for up here," Aunt Thora told Ted. "Then you wouldn't need Mildred."

Ted covered the mannequin's ears. "Bite your tongue. I'll always need Mildred."

"I don't know if a dog would enjoy being cooped up in here," I said, "but a cat might be a good idea."

Chief Fox surveyed the round room. "I think a cat would love it here and the shelter has plenty of them. In fact, there's a beautiful Himalayan there now. You should check her out."

Ted seemed to mull over the suggestion. "I worry about taking on responsibility for another living creature at my age."

"Oh, Ted, you're perfectly healthy," Aunt Thora said. "And you have a lot to offer a feline companion."

"Maybe I could bring her over to play with Candy at your house," Ted said.

"Glory be, no," Aunt Thora said quickly. "Candy would chew her up and pick her teeth with the bones."

I laughed. "She's not exaggerating. Grandma's cat is very territorial."

"Maybe once this fog clears, you can take a ride over to the shelter," Chief Fox said. "Or I could even bring her here for a meet-and-greet."

"That's a wonderful idea," Aunt Thora said.

"Chief, before you go, could I have a quick word?" I asked. I walked him to the top of the spiral staircase. "It's about Miriam Travers. Is there any chance…?"

He held up a hand. "No need to worry about her, Agent Fury. The prosecutor's office has dropped the charges against her."

I clutched my stomach. "Oh, that's a relief."

"I didn't realize you knew her."

"Oh, I don't." I wasn't sure what to say. "I just know her by reputation." I inhaled deeply. "I'm glad everything worked out for the Travers family."

"Everything?" he queried.

"Never mind." I couldn't tell him about my role in getting their retirement money returned to them.

"Where is he?" a voice echoed from the bottom of the stairs. "Where's my husband?"

I heard her panting all the way to the top. Her face was red and she pressed her palm flat against the wall to steady herself.

"Mrs. Rice?" the chief asked.

"Where's Manfred?" she asked. Her gaze darted around the room.

"I'm afraid he's already been taken to the morgue," Chief Fox said.

Mrs. Rice began to sob in earnest.

"I'm so sorry for your loss," I said.

"It seems like a bad dream I'll wake up from," she said. "I mean, I knew Manfred suffered from depression, but I thought we had it under control."

"Did he take medication for his depression?" Chief Fox asked.

"Yes, but…" She stopped.

"But what?" I prompted.

Her eyes widened. "It was full."

Chief Fox and I exchanged glances. "What was full?" he asked.

"His meds," she said absently. "I noticed yesterday but didn't think anything of it. He should have taken a few days' worth at least."

"Are you sure?" I asked. "Maybe he hadn't finished his other bottle yet."

"I'm sure. I pick up the prescriptions for him so I know exactly when he needed to start the next bottle."

"Do you remember which day he should've started?" Chief Fox asked.

"That's easy enough," she replied. "It was the day the fog rolled in. Such an odd thing, isn't it? I've never seen fog like this in all my life."

"Me neither," I said. "And I lived in San Francisco."

Her brow creased. "Why would he have stopped taking his pills without talking to me?"

"That's something he would typically do?" Chief Fox asked.

Her eyes glistened with tears. "Yes, of course. Manfred and I were extremely close. I never wanted him to feel alone in his struggles." She fished a tissue from her pocket and wiped her nose. "I don't understand why he would even come to the lighthouse. He deliberately avoided heights."

"Because he was afraid of them?" I asked.

Her expression darkened. "No, because he didn't trust himself."

Wow. Poor Manfred.

Chief Fox offered her a handkerchief from his pocket. "If you'd like, I can drive you to the morgue so you don't have to go on your own."

Tears streamed down her cheeks. "Would you?"

"Of course." Chief Fox turned to look at me. "Always good

to see you, Agent Fury." He disappeared with Mrs. Rice down the spiraling staircase and I continued to stare after him.

"Earth to Eden," Aunt Thora said. She snapped her fingers. "My darling niece, you have it bad."

I jerked my head toward her. "Have what?"

"Nothing, dear," she said.

"I need to run home and shower before I go back to the office," I said. My day was only just beginning and I wasn't thrilled with its start.

"Thank you for coming on such short notice," Aunt Thora said. "I know I can always count on you."

"That's because you never threaten to…" I almost said 'hex me,' but a quick look at Ted reminded me to end with "punish me."

"Why don't you take Thora with you?" Ted suggested. "I won't be able to leave here to drive her for a while."

"Ted picked me up on the way," Aunt Thora explained. "I wouldn't mind curling up in a ball on the sofa. It isn't every day I see a man fall to his death."

"Come on then," I said. "Let's get you home."

"Drive safely," Ted said. "We don't need any more unfortunate incidents today."

I glanced out the window, thinking about poor Manfred Rice. "No," I said. "We certainly don't."

CHAPTER ELEVEN

AUNT THORA and I arrived back at the house to the sound of my mother and grandmother arguing.

"You'd better knock it off," Grandma said. "I may not be a vengeance demon, but I know more than my share of revenge tactics."

My mother bristled. "For the last time, stop being angry with me over something that happened in a dream. I can't control what you dream about it."

Grandma peered at her closely. "Can't you, though?"

"There are plenty of dream demons who can, but you know perfectly well that I'm a witch like you."

"You sure are," I mumbled.

Grandma shifted her attention to me. Oops. Should've stayed quiet.

"When is that barn going to be finished?" Grandma asked. "Your boyfriend is taking an awfully long time."

"It's a lot of work," I said. "And you know he's not my boyfriend."

"Why not? He's up your alley," Grandma said. "Human. Dull as dishwater. Not an evil bone in his body."

"Not evil at all," my mother said with a vacant smile. "Some very nice bones, in fact. *Very* nice."

"He's not going to bone you with any of his bones, so you may as well move on," Grandma snapped.

My mother looked appalled. "Why would you say such a thing? If we're two consenting adults, what's the harm?"

"He's a carpenter for the barn, not a plumber for your pipes," Grandma said.

I desperately wanted to perform a deaf spell on myself right now. "Can we stop talking about this? John isn't interested in you, Mom. He just wants to focus on the work."

"Only because you spoiled him for me," my mother muttered.

"It was one date," I said. "And we both agreed that we liked each other as friends."

"Can we talk about Manfred Rice?" Aunt Thora asked loudly. She filled the kettle and slammed it on the stovetop with such force that we all flinched.

"Who's that?" my mother asked.

Aunt Thora spun around to face us. "The man who died today," she replied. "Manfred Rice. He fell from the top of the lighthouse."

"Did you know him?" my mother asked.

"No, but I saw him fall," Aunt Thora said. "It was terrible." She paused. "I think it had something to do with the fog."

"You might be right," Grandma said. "Weird things have happened since the fog rolled in. I think it must be supernatural because even my sensible granddaughter's been affected. She thought it was a good idea to dig up my private property."

I bit the inside of my cheek to deter myself from responding.

"I've seen weird things, too," my mother said. "Two women were hitting each other with their handbags over a parking spot. Usually, moments like that warm my cold, dead heart, but they both had children in the car watching the whole unpleasant scene unfold."

I eyed her suspiciously. "Since when do you draw the line at children?"

My mother ignored me.

"Would anyone else like tea?" Aunt Thora asked.

"Which kind?" Grandma walked over to investigate. "I didn't like that hibiscus you used yesterday. It tasted like sweaty armpits."

I cringed. "Thanks for that."

"I won't brew the hibiscus," Aunt Thora promised.

"So why do you think the fog's influence is supernatural?" I asked. "Maybe it's just that the fog is making people feel claustrophobic."

"Eden's right," my mother said. "Any kind of unusual weather event brings out the worst in people. Hurricanes. Floods. Tornadoes. Blackouts. You always end up with looters and hooters."

I shot a quizzical look at my mother. "Say that again? Wait, actually don't say that again."

"You get people breaking into stores—those are the looters, of course," my mother said. "Then you get the people with nothing better to do than spend their time copulating. Boom! The hooters come out."

"People still have access to technology," I argued. "We haven't lost power. It's just hard to see outside."

"You're telling me." Anton appeared in the kitchen. "It took me ages to get home. I thought I'd drop in for lunch and steal time with Ryan." He glanced around. "Where is he?"

"Napping," my mother said. "Charlemagne is curled up around him. They're the picture of sweetness."

"I'll peek in after I eat," Anton said. "I'm starving. What are we having?" He rubbed his hands together.

"Whatever you're making," my mother replied.

Anton grimaced. "Oh, come on. I'm working."

"So are we," I said. "We're figuring out whether the fog is a supernatural event."

Anton opened the fridge and rooted around for something to eat. He pulled out a container and removed the lid. "Would you do the honors?" he asked, holding out the dish for my mother.

My mother zapped the dish with a bolt of magic and steam rose from the stew.

"You're that lazy that you can't even hit a couple buttons on the microwave?" Grandma asked. "Beatrice, you do him no favors by coddling him like that."

Anton grinned, unconcerned. "It's not coddling when it's a mother's love." He retrieved a fork from the drawer and seated himself at the table. "So what are the theories about the fog? A weather spell designed to torture us indefinitely?"

Grandma drummed her short fingernails on the table. "What did you say the jumper's name is again?"

"Manfred Rice," I replied. "Why?"

Grandma took her cup from Aunt Thora's outstretched hand. "I know what this is."

I whipped toward her. "You do?"

She nodded, her face lined with somber wisdom. "Vengeful spirits."

I scowled. "I thought you were serious."

"I am serious," Grandma said. She inhaled the aroma of the tea. "Much better than sweaty armpits."

I took a cup of tea and meandered over to the table. "His wife said he was depressed, but your theory is that a ghost forced him to the top of the lighthouse and then pushed him?"

"Why not?" Grandma replied.

"Revenge for what?" my mother asked. "Blocking his view of the bay?"

"In that case, you'd better stay out of the attic, Mom," Anton said. "Alice might push you out a window for destroying that vegetable garden she started."

"Alice isn't pushing anyone," I said. "She can barely work a TV remote."

Grandma took a sip of tea. "I'm telling you—the shades of murdered mariners have come back to take revenge and they're using the fog to do it."

I folded my arms. "Do you know something about murdered mariners that you're not telling us?"

"I know this story," Anton said. "It's *The Fog*. John Carpenter directed it." He broke into a broad smile. "Awesome movie."

I counted to ten in my head. "Grandma, are you giving me a movie plot as an actual theory?"

Grandma shrugged her bony shoulders. "Why not? Your father and brother are vengeance demons. What's so weird about murdered mariners seeking revenge?"

I closed my eyes. "Are you seriously suggesting that we pursue the plot of *The Fog* as our working theory?"

"Well," Anton said, "there is...fog."

"And dead people," Grandma added.

"Person," I corrected her. "One dead person."

"Do you have a better idea?" my mother asked. She blew out an annoyed breath. "What am I asking? Of course she does. Eden's ideas are always better than anyone else's. Because she's on the side of good and righteousness. Blah blah." She pretended to snore.

I pushed back the chair and stood. "Forget it. I'm going to the office where I can think."

"I'm going to sit on the couch and watch *The Fog*,"

Grandma said. "You should give it a whirl. It's a classic horror movie from the 80's."

"Mom, you know Eden doesn't watch horror movies," my mother said. "Remember that time we tried to get her to watch Halloween? She hid under her bed until we agreed to turn it off."

"Except you only pretended to turn it off," I said. "As soon as I came out, you used a spell to blast it on every wall in the house."

My mother and Grandma cackled and high-fived each other.

"That was incredible," my mother said.

"Nothing against Jamie Lee Curtis," I said, "but I don't like the idea of watching people get murdered for fun."

"They weren't murdered for fun," Anton said. "The killer had his reasons."

I exhaled. "I don't mean he murdered for fun. I mean I don't like murder as entertainment for me. There's enough misery and horror in the world without using it as source material."

"Horror films are vastly underrated," Anton began.

"Says the vengeance demon," I interjected.

"What about Agent Redmond?" my mother asked.

I stopped to look at her. "What about him?"

"Shouldn't he be informed of this latest development?" my mother asked.

"I don't know yet whether there is a development," I replied. "Anyway, he's not the type of agent to accept 'my grandmother saw it in a horror movie' as a reason to act."

"We're only limited by our own imaginations," Grandma said.

"Trust me. If this fog is supernatural, I have every interest in taking care of it," I said. "That's my job."

. . .

I arrived back at the office to find Neville at his desk with a white powdered donut. "Where's Agent Redmond?"

I expected him to be here, ready to issue me a stern reprimand for tardiness.

"He said he'll swing by later," Neville said. "His words."

"Swing by?" I echoed. "How oddly casual of him." At that moment, my phone buzzed. I pulled it out to see a text from Clara. *In love*, it read. There was a heart emoji at the end.

Where are you? I texted back.

Gouda Nuff with Quinn. He never had cheese fries before. Can you believe?

Yes, I typed back. Well, at least I knew where Agent Redmond was. What a slacker.

"What are you working on?" I asked.

Neville jerked his head toward the back table. "A new magical invention. It isn't perfected yet, though, so I'd rather not share the details."

"Sounds interesting." A thought occurred to me. "Did you have to take one of those personality tests?"

"Yes, of course. I'm an ENTP. Not inclined to take a leadership role, but autonomous in my work. We tend to be innovators and inventors."

"So you think the test is really accurate?"

Neville regarded me. "I believe so. Why?"

I told him about sharing the same personality type as my grandmother.

"If there are only sixteen different kinds, odds are you'll be the same as someone in that huge family of yours," Neville said, ever practical. "I would be honored to find out I'm the same type as my grandmother."

"That's because your grandmother is probably a sweetheart," I said. "My grandmother's soul is black, like her coffee."

Neville gave me a sympathetic look. "Agent Fury, it's a

general personality type. It's not a reflection on your moral character."

"I'll try to bear that in mind," I said.

"I heard about the jumper," Neville said. He polished off the rest of his donut. "Terrible tragedy." His cheeks puffed as he chewed and his mouth remained dusted with white powder.

"It is a tragedy, but I'm not sure it's the kind of tragedy we think it is." I turned on the computer and typed in search terms for historic shipwrecks in this area.

"You're using the computer," Neville said.

"Very observant." Hmm. There were more results than I bargained for.

"If you're looking for solitaire, there's an icon…"

I swiveled in my chair to face him. "I'm not playing a game, Neville. I'm working. My grandmother thinks Manfred Rice didn't fall or commit suicide. She thinks there's something supernatural at work."

"Ah, like what?"

I debated whether to share her theory. "She thinks the fog is caused by murdered mariners bent on revenge."

His lips puckered. "Ooh, as in *The Fog*."

"Am I the only one who doesn't know the movie?"

"You really should watch it. A brilliant film."

"Well, now I'm researching shipwrecks along the coast of Chipping Cheddar to see if there's any truth to the theory."

"There have been an awful lot of strange occurrences due to the fog," Neville said. "The police scanner is three times as busy as normal. They haven't seemed to be of a magical nature, though, so I haven't paid close attention."

"I guess you should start," I said. "Do me a favor and look up local shipwrecks on your computer. Start from the bottom of the list and I'll start from the top."

"An excellent and efficient plan, Agent Fury."

"Thank you. Once in a while, I pull through with a reasonable suggestion."

After a deep dive into local shipwrecks, I came up with a single possibility. The Brizo.

"Who knew history would come in handy in my line of work?" I asked.

"It's like mathematics," Neville said. "We all think we don't use it when we all do."

"Speak for yourself," I said. "I don't math."

"Math isn't a verb, Agent Fury."

The *Lord of the Rings* theme song played out of my backside. I retrieved my phone from the pocket. "A text from Agent Redmond."

Neville frowned. "Why *Lord of the Rings*?"

"He looks like Legolas with short hair."

Neville smiled. "He does, actually. Good call, Agent Fury."

"Eden." I scanned the text and laughed. "Sweet Hecate. He's playing hooky."

"What do you mean?"

"He's telling me he's sick in his B&B when Clara told me they're at the diner together." I took a screenshot and sent it to Clara.

"That seems unlike him," Neville said.

"Hey, when you're smitten, you're smitten," I said. I knew the feeling, not that I could act on it.

I turned off my sun lamp and the computer.

"Off to play a little hooky yourself?" Neville asked.

"No, I'm going to do more research, but my source is at home."

"It's not online?" he asked.

"Not this one." I waved to him over my shoulder. "I'll be in touch when I know something."

. . .

112

I arrived home and snuck inside and up to the attic before anyone noticed me. I didn't want to endure Grandma's hostile glowering. I found Alice on my mattress, her eyes were glued to the television.

"I see you've discovered *Pride and Prejudice*," I said.

Alice didn't bother to tear her gaze from the screen. "If only there'd been men like Mr. Darcy around when I was an eligible young woman."

I flopped beside her. "Same."

Alice shot me a quizzical look. "What's the matter?"

I curled around the pillow. "You were here when the town was first settled. Do you remember anything about a ship called the Brizo?"

Alice vanished, a sure sign that she did, in fact, remember something.

"Alice, come back," I said. "I need to know more about this ship. It might be connected to the fog."

Alice returned, but not to the mattress. Instead, she hovered a safe distance away. "Why do you think that?"

"I read an article about the shipwreck today," I said. "There wasn't a lot of information, though. I thought you might know something since it was during your lifetime."

Alice floated to perch on the edge of the mattress. "I'll never forget that ship, not as long as I live." She paused. "I mean, exist."

I sat up, hugging the pillow, interested to hear her version of events. "What happened?"

"There'd been a vicious storm. The ship entered the bay seeking shelter. Patrick O'Neill had been in charge of the lighthouse at the time. He was the first to spot the ship and alerted Arthur Davenport."

"So what happened?"

"Arthur sent someone out to meet the ship and discovered there was yellow fever on board," Alice explained.

"So permission was refused," I said.

"Of course," Alice said. "We couldn't risk infecting everyone in town. It was a dangerous disease. It would have wiped out our entire population."

"Did they come ashore anyway?" I asked.

Alice drifted over to the window. "They tried, but some of the men in town intercepted them."

"Intercepted them how?" I didn't like where this was going.

Alice gave me a dark look. "The townsmen sank their dinghy and, when two of the men from the dinghy tried to swim to shore, they were killed."

I flinched. "Oh, Alice. That's awful."

"It was," Alice said. "They were infected with yellow fever, though. I don't know what else could have been done. The risk was too great."

"What happened to the rest of the people on the ship?" I asked.

"The ship sank during the storm and everyone aboard drowned."

I covered my face with my hands. "Great balls of fury, Alice. No wonder you've never forgotten. It's traumatizing."

"We held a vigil for the dead," Alice said. "The men who sank the dinghy—they spoke. As good Puritans, I know they wrestled with what they'd done." She shook her head. "Poor Jerome Rice. He died the next winter, leaving a wife and three kids. She was convinced that the crew of the Brizo had cursed her husband before they died."

I blinked. "Did you say Rice?"

She faced me. "That's right. His wife was Penelope. A lovely woman."

My head was spinning. "They had three children."

"Yes. Amazingly, they all lived to adulthood. You know

how it was back then," Alice said. "We all lost children." Her expression grew sorrowful.

"Do you happen to know whether Manfred Rice is a descendant of Jerome?" He had to be.

"I would assume so," Alice said. "It's like the O'Neills, the Davenports, the Danforths. All of those people are descended from us, the original inhabitants."

I couldn't believe Grandma's movie theory could actually be correct. Were shades from the ship called the Brizo finally exacting their revenge on the descendants of their murderers? And why now?

"Manfred died today," I said. "He fell from the top of the lighthouse."

Alice gasped. "How awful. Why was he up there?"

"Presumably to kill himself," I said, "but now I'm not so sure. I need to do a little more digging." In the meantime, I'd need the names of anyone else involved in the sinking of the ship. "Do you remember the names of the other men who rowed out to meet the dinghy?"

Alice squeezed her eyes closed, thinking hard. "I can see them in my mind's eye, but Jerome is the only one I remember specifically. I was friends with Penelope, you see."

As much as I wanted to take a nap, I pulled myself to my feet.

"You're leaving again?" Alice asked. "What about Mr. Darcy?"

"He's all yours, Alice. I need to get to the library." I was glad Agent Redmond was distracted by Clara because I had actual work to do.

CHAPTER TWELVE

I HADN'T BEEN BACK to the local library since my return to Chipping Cheddar. Now that I was in the building, I felt guilty about it. The library had been a staple of my youth. The place I sought refuge when my family life became intolerable. When my grandmother hexed me with hairy arms and legs in the middle of summer because I flushed her blood supply for black magic down the toilet, the library was a safe haven. Even in high school, when I caught Tanner cheating on me, I came here and hid between the stacks. If anyone caught me crying, it was easy enough to blame the book I was reading rather than my unhappy life.

"Eden Fury? It can't be."

I smiled at the older woman behind the counter. Her hair was streaked with gray and the style of her glasses had changed, but I'd recognize Helen Halbe anywhere. The librarian was a fixture here. I suspected she had a cot in the back where she slept because she never seemed to be anywhere else.

"Hello, Mrs. Halbe. It's so good to see you again." Mrs. Halbe isn't your typical librarian. She doesn't shush anyone

116

or judge anyone's reading material. And she hosts as many events at the library she can reasonably fit on the calendar.

She peered at me over the rim of her glasses. "You haven't aged a day, except your boobs look a little bigger. Did you have a boob job in California? I hear all the women have breast augmentation there."

I approached the counter. "It's probably just the bra I'm wearing."

"Well, buy one in another color because it's working for you," she said.

"How's Mr. Halbe?" I asked.

She waved a hand. "Oh, you know Ethan. As long as he has his gardening shears, he's a happy camper." She dropped her voice to a whisper. "I hear you're a secret agent now."

"It's not actually secret. I work for the FBI in the cyber crimes division. My office is over on Asiago Street."

She wrinkled her nose at the mention of the seedy area in town. "Can't you request a better location?"

"You know how inflexible government budgets can be," I said.

Mrs. Halbe surveyed the library. "You bet I do. We've had more cuts than I care to count. I had to switch a couple paid part-time positions to volunteers."

I sucked in a breath. "Ooh, I'm sorry."

She brightened. "We make it work. I still aim to make this a gathering place for the community. We've got computers. We offer e-books. You can borrow online." She shrugged. "I have no interest in letting the library become an ancient relic."

"You do a great job," I said. "Speaking of ancient relics, that's kind of why I'm here."

Her brow lifted. "Really? If I recall your literary tastes correctly, you preferred the ones with Fabio on the cover."

My cheeks flashed with heat. "Those were for my mother.

She didn't like to check them out herself, so she made me do it. I liked young adult fantasy books."

She aimed a finger at me. "That's right. You were one of those Potterheads, weren't you?"

"I enjoyed the books," I said vaguely. How could I explain to Mrs. Halbe that I often imagined I was Lord Voldemort's daughter later adopted by the Weasleys? It was one of my favorite forms of escape.

"And now you need the history section?" she asked.

"Local history," I said. "Anything that references the Brizo. It was a ship that tried to come to port, but there were passengers infected with…"

"Yellow fever," she interrupted. "Yes, I recall the story." Her expression clouded over. "A terrible tragedy that the town prefers not to remember."

My fingers curled around the edge of the counter. "You know about it?"

Mrs. Halbe nodded. "I don't think you'll find much here, I'm afraid. People were forbidden from writing about it, so there was no official record. Anything that had been written was destroyed."

"Except I found a reference to the Brizo online," I said. "It didn't say much. Just listed as one of the shipwrecks nearby."

"Yes, that makes sense. The shipwreck itself is documented, but not the details as to why or how it happened. I suspect there was no reference to the murder of those who tried to swim to shore either."

"How do you know about that?" I asked. "If people weren't allowed to keep a written record, how do the stories get preserved?"

"Do you know how many elderly people still use the library?" she asked. "Quite a lot, as it happens. And they've been coming here since before you were born. I'm a talker. Everybody in town knows that."

I smiled. "One of your distinguishing characteristics as a librarian."

"I love stories. I don't care if they're oral or written. When people come here with a good tale, I listen."

"And you remember stories about the Brizo?"

"You don't forget a story like that one." She shook her head. "Children died on that ship. Those people only wanted refuge from the storm."

"And the townspeople at the time decided to prevent it?"

"There was a vote, from what I understand," Mrs. Halbe said. "The council members at the time voted as to whether to let them come ashore."

"But they decided the risk was too great?"

She nodded. "Chipping Cheddar is a small town. It was even smaller then. Imagine the damage a disease like yellow fever could do. We probably wouldn't be standing here now if they'd come ashore."

"So you agree with what they did?"

Mrs. Halbe inhaled deeply, contemplating the question. "It's a tough one. I'll say that much. I don't agree with cold-blooded murder, but I do agree with refusing entry. They're not responsible for destroying the ship. That was Mother Nature's doing."

"But they are responsible for killing those who tried to swim to shore."

Her mouth formed a thin line. "I've heard that, but I'm not sure whether that part is true. It could have been an effort to malign some of the more prominent families in town."

Oh, wow. I hadn't considered that as a possibility. "Slander?"

Mrs. Halbe glanced around the library before answering. "You know there were rivalries, especially among the cheese-

119

makers. Some of them made a conscious effort to damage the reputations of others."

"Because of cheese?" The lengths people were willing to go to...

Mrs. Halbe nodded. "You have to remember, Eden. Cheese was a critical part of this town's economic success. Many a family acquired their wealth as a result of their popularity. Torpedoing a rival's reputation...It wasn't unheard of."

But Alice knew. Well, she knew Jerome's name, so at least that much was true.

"Thanks for all your help, Mrs. Halbe," I said.

"You're not going to check anything out today?"

"Not right now," I said. "Unfortunately, the only time I have for reading is in connection with the investigation I'm working on."

"Good luck to you. Don't be a stranger."

I looked around the familiar interior of the library and felt a sense of comfort. "I definitely won't. It feels good to be back."

And, for the first time since my arrival, I actually meant it.

I returned home from the library and walked smack into the middle of an argument between my mother and grandmother. Talk about a rock and a hard place.

"It was your turn to watch Ryan," my mother said heatedly. "I told you I had to go to the store."

"It wasn't," Grandma insisted. "You said you were going to take him with you."

Ryan sat in the recliner, gnawing on one of Charlemagne's toys.

"Ryan is fine," I said. "He just has a little scrape on his chin."

"And do you think your sister-in-law will be so nonchalant about it?" my mother demanded. "Verity will likely say he needs stitches and make a big deal about having to use her druid healing powers, like it's such a burden."

"Sounds like someone else we know who's standing so close I can smell the toothpaste she used on her zits this morning," Grandma said.

"I don't have any zits," I said. I resisted the urge to touch my face and search for signs of a new one. "I only used toothpaste to brush my teeth."

"Really?" Grandma said. "Then how do you explain your breath?"

Someone was clearly still angry with me about the burnbook.

"Grandma is right," my mother said.

"About my breath?" I breathed into my hand and sniffed it.

"No," my mother said, "that Verity is almost as annoying as you."

"You're both being ridiculous." Trying to reason with my family was like trying to reason with a troop of mushrooms.

"I'm in the clear," my mother said, jabbing a finger at herself. "You're the one who let him walk without holding his hand."

"That's how they learn," Grandma said. "You would know that if you ever stopped coddling Anton."

"I do not coddle Anton. He's a grown man."

Tempers flared and I felt the energy in the room shift. Ryan started to cry and threw the python's toy on the floor.

"See what you did!" my mother fumed. "My grandson is in tears because of you."

"Your grandson is in tears because he has you for a grandmother," Grandma shot back.

"Take that back," my mother said.

An aura of darkness surrounded each of them. I backed against the wall and inched closer to Ryan in case he needed a protective bubble.

I felt a charge of electricity and braced myself. Things were about to get ugly.

"Don't you dare," Grandma said in a low voice.

Too late.

My mother drew first. She aimed her finger and said, "By the power of Nyx, I draw from the heavens and punish you!"

A thunderbolt tore through the family room. I huddled over Ryan to shield him. I watched as Grandma lit up like a tacky Christmas tree. Her hair stood on end and her body fizzled. She wobbled twice before keeling over.

"Are you seriously resorting to lightning strikes?" I yelled. "You're arguing over a cut on his chin that didn't even bleed."

Lightning strikes were generally reserved for more serious offenses. Not that I approved of them then either.

Ryan stopped crying and burped.

Grandma remained sprawled across the floor, her body smoking.

"Did you really have to smite her?" I asked.

"It isn't technically smiting and you know it," my mother said.

I pulled a face. "Not really the point," I said. "This was completely unnecessary." I never agreed with killing each other, but today's reasons were far flimsier than normal.

We stared at Grandma's body until it was no longer twitching or smoking.

"She looks so peaceful when she's dead," my mother said.

"Can you revive her, please?"

"Why? Can't we just enjoy the silence a little longer?"

I counted to ten in my head. "She's not getting any younger, Mom. One of these days, you may not be able to bring her back."

My mother blew a raspberry. "Who are you kidding? That old witch is as long-lasting as Styrofoam. She's not going anywhere."

Ryan climbed down from the chair and toddled over to Grandma's body to inspect her. My mother and I waited to see what he would do. His cheeks puffed and he made a sound.

"What's he doing?" my mother asked.

I smiled. "He's cooling her off. Blowing off the steam like we do with our tea."

My mother made a delighted sound. "Isn't he a clever boy?"

Ryan poked Grandma's shoulder. I scooped him up and smoothed back his fine hair. "She'll be fine in a minute. Mom-mom will fix her right up." I glared at my mother. "Won't you, Mom-mom?"

"Fine," my mother huffed. "But she had it coming." She invoked Nyx again and brought my grandmother back from death.

Grandma staggered to her feet and coughed. Her face was black and her eyes were slightly bulging. She looked down and noticed a burn on the corner of the rug.

"Look what you did to my favorite rug," Grandma said. "That's from Pottery Barn."

My mother shrugged, unconcerned. "Worth it."

Grandma gasped in horror. "I'll show you what's worth it, you ungrateful spawn..."

Before she could raise a magical finger, I jumped between them and spread out my arms as though trying to herd Velociraptors. "Enough!"

Ryan burst into laughter. Both mother and grandmother jerked their heads toward him.

"You liked that, Ryan?" my mother asked.

He clapped and smiled, then sat on the rug and poked his finger in the scorched hole.

"He liked the lightning," I said. "It doesn't mean he liked what you did with it."

Grandma moved closer to crouch beside him. "Would you like to learn to do that? We can teach you."

"You will not!" I was aghast. "He's only one. You can't let a child wield power like that."

"We would've let you, if you'd shown any interest," my mother said.

"He would kill someone that he wouldn't be able to bring back from the dead," I said. "It's not the same as doing it to each other." And even that was a macabre practice I wanted no part of.

"Typical Eden," my mother said, rolling her eyes.

"E," Ryan said, and pointed to me.

"He finally knows who you are," my mother said. "That's progress."

"What do you mean? He knows me."

"We'd been showing him photos of you while you lived in California," my mother said, "but we weren't sure whether he'd remember."

"I've been here for weeks now," I said. "I think he's getting to know me because I've been spending time with him."

"As a good aunt should," Grandma said. "I logged lots of hours with my nieces and nephews when they were younger and look how they turned out."

"Are you suggesting that Uncle Moyer is a lawyer because of the time you spent with him as a child?" I asked.

Grandma put her hands on her hips. "Do you have a better theory?"

"I'm taking Princess Buttercup for a walk," I said, eager to get away. I whistled for the hellhound.

"At least her saliva can cut through the fog," Grandma said.

"I'm not going to have her spread demonic acid around just to see better," I said. "If I'm not back in time for dinner, eat without me."

"I'm not even thinking about dinner," Grandma said. "All I can think about is this poor rug."

"You should've thought of that before you annoyed me," my mother replied.

"Next time, aim for something you don't mind ruining, like those drapes." Grandma gestured to the windows. "Burning those would be an improvement."

I hurried from the room before the situation escalated again. Princess Buttercup waited for me by the door, as though sensing the urgency to leave the house.

"Let's get out of here before someone calls the fire department," I said.

The hellhound barked in agreement.

CHAPTER THIRTEEN

IF ANYONE HAD their finger on the pulse of Chipping Cheddar's oral history, it was the Graces. I'd seen Aggie at the supernatural council meetings, of course, but not her sisters. I spent many childhood hours soaking up their good energy to offset the darkness at home. Anton went through a particularly demonic stage in his teens—a hormonal vengeance demon isn't the big brother anyone dreams of. One time, he was so angry with me for using his computer without asking that he channeled his rage into a cloud of dust that followed me around like Charlie Brown's friend Pig Pen. It was so embarrassing and impossible to explain to my mostly human classmates. The supernaturals among them thought it was hilarious. Clara avoided me because my emotional energy became too volatile. She couldn't handle being too close to me without risking overstimulation. I ended up agreeing to wash my dad's car for the next six months to get him to remove the cloud.

"Eden, thank the gods." Thalia Grace answered the door in a white silk robe and her titian hair styled in a French twist. "I was beginning to think you'd decided to shun us."

She stroked the top of the hellhound's head. "And so wonderful to see you again, Princess Buttercup."

I crossed the threshold into their glamorous foyer with its black and white checkered tiles and sweeping staircase. The exterior gave no hint of the incredibly stylish interior.

"I'm so sorry it took so long. I have no excuse."

The most beautiful of the three sisters kissed my cheek, leaving a stain of red lipstick behind. "Nonsense," Thalia said. "Aggie told us that you've been spinning your wheels since the moment you arrived in town. All is forgiven." She crooked a finger. "Follow me into the courtyard. My sisters and I are working on a little art project for the gallery."

I walked to the back of the house and entered the open space. Where a regular human house might have a back patio, the Graces had a private oasis. In addition to the craft table and four stools painted in bright turquoise, there was a pond, a copse, plentiful flowers, and birdsong. It was one of the most peaceful places in Chipping Cheddar and they didn't need to leave the house to enjoy it.

"Oh, Eden. What a delightful surprise." Charity hurried over to kiss me on each cheek. "You are a sight for sore eyes, sweetie." Charity was shorter and bustier than her sisters, but her skin was every bit as porcelain and unblemished. Humans in town attributed the Graces' youthful, glowing skin to a secret beauty cream.

"I've missed you all," I said.

Aggie stood at a craft table, holding an ear of corn. "I've been patiently waiting for you to turn up on our doorstep. I knew it was only a matter of time."

"At least I see you at the council meetings," I said. Although it wasn't quite the same as enjoying their company in a social setting. Aggie wore her official hat at the meetings.

"Yes, this is much better." She inclined her head toward a

pitcher of iced tea on the table. "Would you like a cold drink?"

"No, thanks." I spotted a plethora of vegetables on the craft table. "So what's the art project?" I asked. The Graces were forever in the middle of a creative endeavor. Most walls in their house were covered in murals they painted themselves.

Aggie smiled. "We'll show you."

Two bluebirds chirped as they swooped down to untie the silken sash of Thalia's robe. The white material slipped off, leaving a naked Thalia in the middle of the courtyard.

"We're designing a new kind of scarecrow," Charity said. "Out of vegetables."

"Based on my body," Thalia added.

I could see why. Thalia was built like a fertility goddess.

"The theme is 'you are what you eat,'" Aggie added.

"Um, won't the food attract the animals you're trying to keep away?" I asked.

"Since when do we create anything for practical use, darling?" Charity said. "It's art."

"Of course."

"The head will be this pumpkin," Aggie said. She touched the stem of the pumpkin. "And we'll use linked corn cobs for legs."

"Which do you think for the breasts?" Charity asked. "I think watermelons are too large and will topple the scarecrow."

Thalia patted her chest. "I agree. It's a veggie sculpture of me, not you, Charity."

Aggie sighed. "Fine. Go with the cantaloupes."

Princess Buttercup sniffed the food on the table.

"Not for you," I said firmly and the hellhound slunk away.

"Any thoughts on when this fog will end?" Charity asked. "My sisters and I have a betting pool."

"That's sort of the reason I'm here," I said. I perched on one of the turquoise stools. "I take it you've heard about Manfred Rice?"

"The lighthouse jumper from this morning?" Thalia asked.

"Yes," I replied. "I think his death might be connected to the fog." I explained what I'd learned about the Brizo.

"I remember that incident," Aggie said.

My head snapped toward her. "You were here?" I knew they were old, but I didn't remember they were around so early in the town's history.

"No, but we arrived not long after," Aggie said. "Charity had met a sea merchant who said he lived here and she decided to find him."

Charity sighed at the memory. "That was Edwin Reynolds. I followed him here from England."

"And you've been here ever since?" I asked. "You must've really liked it."

The sisters exchanged knowing smiles. "We've fought from time to time over whether we should move on, but we're comfortable here," Aggie said.

"In a good way," Charity added. "Not complacent."

"Anyway, I heard the story from Jerome himself in the tavern not long before he died," Aggie said. "It stayed with me."

"I guess so," I said. "It's awful."

"So you think the spirits want revenge?" Charity asked. "Why now, after all this time?"

"No idea," I said. "I'm trying to get to the bottom of it and see what I can piece together." And see if I could make it stop before anyone else got hurt.

"If it truly is vengeful spirits, then you should visit any descendants at risk," Thalia said. "I'd start with any Travers and Seamans. Do a protective spell on their homes or something."

I froze. "Did you say Travers?"

"That's right," Thalia said. "Milton Travers was with Jerome and Sigmund Seaman when they rowed out to meet the dinghy."

That might explain why Simon's poker game had gotten out of hand. Somehow the ghosts cursed Simon so that he lost all his money. Maybe they assumed it would drive him to suicide like Manfred. They obviously didn't count on my interference.

"Didn't they serve on the council at the time?" Aggie asked.

"Yes," Thalia said. "They voted to refuse entry and felt it was only right that they should be the ones to handle it personally. They considered themselves honorable men."

"So you think the ghosts of the drowned passengers have created this fog as part of their revenge on the town?" Charity asked.

"It serves as a literal smoke screen," Thalia added.

"Well, Sidrach Seaman is still alive," Charity said. "I know him from one of the organizations I'm involved in. A grumpy old thing, but he doesn't deserve to be murdered by ghosts for something his great-great whatever did."

"Sigmund and Sidrach?" I said. "They sound like the names of sleestaks from *Land of the Lost*."

Thalia laughed. "Your references have always been so oblique. I'm glad to see you haven't changed."

"That's what happens when you grow up hiding in your room with a television for company," I said.

Charity gave me a proud smile. "Well, you're clearly not hiding anymore."

No, I wasn't, although there were still moments when I

wanted to. "Okay, so I've got Rice, Travers, Seaman. Was anyone else directly involved?"

"Not to my knowledge," Thalia said.

"Well, Travers is still alive, albeit bruised by a rolling pin," I said. "I'll have my assistant set up a protective ward around his house, just to be on the safe side."

"Sidrach lives on Provolone Lane," Charity said. "Try not to take his grumpy attitude personally. He's like that with everyone."

I shot her a look. "You do remember where I live, don't you? I think I'm equipped to handle one grumpy old man."

The Graces laughed.

"You're welcome to hide out here anytime, Eden," Thalia said.

"Thanks," I said. A memory of the burnbook flashed in my mind. "I just might need to take you up on that."

Provolone Lane was only a few blocks away from Munster Close, so I dropped Princess Buttercup back at the house and continued on foot to Sidrach Seaman's house. Through the haze, I spotted a figure in a rocking chair on the front porch.

"Mr. Seaman?" I asked.

The elderly man swung his head in my direction. His head was bald and a puff of white covered his chin, reminding me of a cloud.

"You're on my lawn," he said.

"Am I?" I glanced down to see that I was. "Well, it's easier to talk to you from this distance than standing on the sidewalk."

He scrunched his face. "And what makes you think I want to talk to you?"

"I get the sense that you don't," I replied, "but I'm here to help you."

"I don't want any lululemon," he said, and jutted out his chin.

Stubborn fool. This one wouldn't be easy. "Do I look like I sell leggings?"

"Not in that outfit, but you look like you're selling something. What is it? Tupperware? No, wait. I bet it's new windows." He pointed his cane at me. "I don't need new windows."

"Mr. Seaman, I'm not here to sell you anything. I need to talk to you about one of your ancestors, Sigmund Seaman."

His chest puffed. "The jewel in our crown. What about him?"

Slowly, I approached the porch. "Do you know about his involvement with a ship called the Brizo?"

Sidrach stroked his white beard. "Name doesn't ring a bell. Was it a cheese ship?"

I cocked my head. "A cheese ship? I don't think there was any such thing as a cheese ship."

"Sure there was." He spat on the porch. "How do you think all that cheese got here back then?"

"I'm pretty sure the cheese came from the local dairy farms," I said.

"Poppycock," he said. He shook his cane at me. "That's one of those conspiracy theories."

"There's a conspiracy over whether the cheese was domestic or imported?"

"Of course there is. Do you live under a rock?"

I drew a deep breath. "Mr. Seaman, Sigmund was one of the townspeople responsible for refusing entry to the passengers of a ship called the Brizo."

"So what? No one got their cheese shipments that month? Boo hoo."

"Every passenger on board the ship died," I said. I continued to stand there, waiting for the news to sink in.

"Well, I wasn't there, was I? I'm old, but I'm not that old."

How could I explain the situation to him in a way that he could understand? "Mr. Seaman, do you believe in ghosts?"

His wrinkled face paled. "What's this about, young lady? Are you trying to frighten me out of my house? You want to buy my land for cheap, don't you? Build a strip mall or one of those hobby shops filled with painted figurines."

Oh boy. "No, Mr. Seaman. I don't want to do any of those things."

"Well, good because you won't get my land to do it with. This property has been in my family for generations and it's going to stay that way."

"Do any other members of your family live in town, Mr. Sidrach?"

"Why do you want to know? So you can pit them against me?" He slapped his thigh. "Joke's on you. They all moved to North Carolina years ago, left me here all alone." He paused. "Just the way I like it."

Just the way they like it, too, I suspected. At least I knew he was the only one I had to protect in Chipping Cheddar. I decided to take a different tack. I took a step closer and produced my badge.

"Mr. Seaman, due to the fog, we're offering all residents over the age of seventy free transportation to Miami until the weather clears. The air quality has been deemed too dangerous." I was careful to make it an offer rather than a mandate. I had a feeling Sidrach automatically pushed back against any direct order.

"Miami?" He rocked in his chair. "I went to Miami once. Lots of half naked women with their butts hanging out."

"Maybe we can have you redirected to…"

He rose to his feet, using his cane to stay upright. "Where do I sign up?"

"I can make the arrangements for you." And by me, I meant Neville.

"Have you asked my friend Joe yet? He's eighty and he's always up for a good time."

"What's Joe's last name?"

"Hever."

"I'll make sure we get in touch with him so you can travel together." I'd feel better if Sidrach had a companion anyway.

He cracked a smile. "I knew it would be a lucky day. I found a penny under the sofa cushion this morning."

"Oh, were you hunting for the TV remote?"

He frowned. "No, my teeth." He tapped his mouth. "Found 'em."

"I'll send a courier over with all the information," I said. The sooner I could get him out of town and away from the vengeful mariners, the better.

"I hope there are single ladies in our hotel," he said. "It'd be convenient to have a room right there."

"I bet there will be. Miami is a popular city."

"The odds are in my favor then. I'd better go and pack. I've got a banana hammock that hasn't seen the sun since 1977." Despite his cane, I noticed a spring in Sidrach's step as he opened the door and disappeared inside.

I hurried away from the house and called Neville to make the arrangements. If I had to book a trip for every resident in potential danger, then so be it. Anything to spare them Manfred's cruel fate. What happened to the Brizo passengers was tragic, but I couldn't let their ghosts wreak havoc in town—not on my watch. If vengeful spirits were responsible for the fog and its deadly side effects, then it was time to lift their curse once and for all.

CHAPTER FOURTEEN

"I APPRECIATE you taking us out here," I said. "I know it's tough with the fog."

I'd decided to take the bull by the horns and confront the spirits of the Brizo. That meant I needed a boat. Good thing I knew a carpenter with a very nice one.

"I can't work on the barn under these conditions," John said. "Might as well make myself useful some other way."

"We would've waited for the fog to clear, but Quinn is only in town for a few more days," I said. When Agent Redmond discovered my plan, he'd insisted on accompanying me to monitor my performance. I wasn't thrilled with the oversight but didn't see any way out of it.

"The whole purpose of my visit is to learn more about this forgotten slice of history," Agent Redmond lied.

"Funny, I was beginning to think the whole purpose of your visit was to woo my best friend." Oops. I hadn't intended to say that out loud.

Agent Redmond scowled but said nothing.

"So you're looking for the wreckage?" John peered over

135

the side of the boat, but it was impossible to see anything in the thick fog.

"Yes." Unfortunately, I couldn't be totally upfront with John. He knew nothing about the supernatural world and I wasn't about to break rule number one in front of Agent Redmond.

John faced us. "Don't you guys need equipment or something? You're not going to see a darn thing like this."

"I've got it covered." I produced a small tin container from my pocket. "Mint?"

"Don't mind if I do." John popped the mint into his mouth and began to chew. I watched carefully as his alert expression faded.

"John?" I waved a hand in front of his face. No response. "I'm sorry to do this to you, friend, but it's necessary. You have a seat here and everything will be fine." I guided him to a seating platform and made sure he was comfortable.

"Nicely done, Agent Fury."

"That's because I'm not incompetent," I said.

"No one is claiming you are," Agent Redmond said. "Now, how do you plan to summon the ghosts?"

I strode to the side of the boat. "Watch and learn." I cleared my throat so that I could project my voice. "Daughters of Poseidon and Amphitrite, hear me." The boat began to rock as the waves rolled underneath. "I seek your wisdom and guidance."

I squinted into the fog, hoping to catch a glimpse of a fin—any sign of mermaids or other supernatural sea creatures.

"You might need to try…"

I stopped him with a sharp look. "I'm not finished yet." I shifted my attention back to the water. "Nymphs, selkies, I beseech you…"

"No need to beseech," a voice called back. "We're here. You just can't see us through this ridiculous fog."

I leaned over the side and saw the bobbing head of a mermaid. "Thank you for answering my call."

"Hey, I know it's not easy to get our attention. We don't have the internet or anything, as cool as that would be." The mermaid smiled up at me. "The name's Clarissa."

"Eden," I said.

Agent Redmond appeared beside me and the mermaid perked up.

"Well, hello Mr. Handsome," Clarissa said. "If you're interested in trading those legs for fins, just say the word. I know a sea witch who can help."

"He's happy in his current form," I said.

Clarissa flipped onto her back. "How can we serve you?"

"I'm looking for the wreckage of a ship that sank here," I said. "It's called the Brizo."

"I know exactly where that is," Clarissa said. "My sisters and I have tea parties there sometimes. It's fairly intact."

"It's nearby?" I asked.

"Sure is. Would you like us to take you there?"

What a relief. "I would."

"You'd better have a seat then," Clarissa said. "We'll steer your boat from down here. It'll be easier."

"Thanks, I'd appreciate it." Since the captain of my boat was currently catatonic.

I sat beside John and checked to make sure he was still breathing. Agent Redmond sat beside me.

"I don't see why the ship's current location is relevant," Agent Redmond said.

"Patience, grasshopper."

I felt the boat turn as the mermaids pushed it through the water. It was impossible to see anything through the fog, so I sat tight until Clarissa called my name.

I returned to the side of the boat. "We're here?"

"It's directly below you," Clarissa confirmed.

I removed a small jar from my handbag and opened the lid. To the untrained eye, it looked like glitter. As I tipped the jar, the boat began to rock. Agent Redmond grabbed me by the waist and my foot slipped, causing me to drop the jar. Colorful dust exploded all over the deck.

"Hey!" I said.

"I didn't want you to fall," Agent Redmond said.

"And I didn't want this to fall." I gestured to the magic dust now scattered across the deck. I'd intended to sprinkle it over the water so that I had a clear view of the ship's final resting place.

Agent Redmond stared at the mess on the deck. "Have I ruined the summoning?"

I bristled with annoyance. "Not for lack of trying." I leaned over the side. "Clarissa, would you mind bringing me a piece of the ship? A small sample is fine."

Clarissa dove to the bottom and returned with a fragment of wood. She tossed it onto the boat. "Will this work?"

I retrieved the piece from the deck and examined it. It included the letter 'z' from Brizo. "This is perfect. Thank you."

"What do you intend to do with it?" Clarissa asked.

"Summon a spirit or two," I replied. Or thirty.

Clarissa shuddered. "They won't be pleasant, not with the deaths they suffered."

"It's not a social call."

"If you need nothing more from us, I think we'll be on our way," Clarissa said. "Good luck." Her head disappeared beneath the waves and her fin slapped the surface of the water before following suit.

"What now?" Agent Redmond asked.

"Take a seat," I said. "I don't need you to mess up this next part."

I took a shaker from my handbag and sprinkled salt in a

circle around the deck and placed the fragment of the ship in the middle. Then I created a second circle with rune rocks and sat cross-legged in the center.

"You didn't name summoning as one of your skills," Agent Redmond said. There was an accusatory note in his voice.

"I'm not trying to hide anything," I said. "Sometimes I only realize I can do something when I actually need to do it. It's called rising to the occasion."

I focused my energy and began to chant.

"Shades of the Brizo, I summon thee," I said. "Make your presence known."

A gust of wind blew across the deck and I shut my eyes to protect them from debris. When I opened them again, the salt circle was packed with gaunt spirits dressed in transparent rags.

"Who calls upon the Brizo?" Based on the style of the hat, it appeared to be the captain speaking.

"I do." I rose to my feet. "My name is Eden Fury and I am tasked with protecting this town."

The captain directed his gaze toward land. "Chipping Cheddar?"

"Yes," I replied.

The captain spat on the deck, or would have, if he'd been in his physical form. "A curse be upon that town."

"Is it?" I asked.

The captain swung his head back toward me. "Is what?"

"Is there a curse on the town?" I asked. "Did you create this never-ending fog to mask your attack?"

The captain bellowed. "I wish I had that kind of power. I would relish the opportunity to take my revenge upon those who wronged us."

"It's true then?" I asked. "What happened to you?"

"Aye, it's true," the captain said. "We were stricken with illness and sought refuge from a storm. Those in charge refused us entry. Some of us tried to row ashore in secret to seek help for the sick, but we were found out and intercepted."

"And you perished?"

"Not all at once," the captain said. "Some took longer than others."

"Drowning is not a merciful way to die," a crew member interrupted.

"Silence, Hansen," the captain said. "I am in charge of this discourse."

Hansen lowered his head and fell silent.

"So you haven't unleashed this fog on the town as part of a revenge plan?" I asked.

"If I had such abilities, I would have unleashed them a long time ago," the captain replied.

I glanced helplessly at Agent Redmond, who only shrugged.

"If it's any consolation," I said, "I apologize on behalf of the town for what was done to you."

The captain nodded crisply. "Aye, it was a tragedy, and we've continued to suffer in our watery graves ever since."

"We weren't given decent burials," Hansen chimed in.

"Hansen!" the captain said sharply.

"Your bodies are still down there?" I asked.

"What the fish and time haven't picked clean," the captain replied.

"I'll tell you what," I began, "now that we know its location, I'll do my best to make sure that your ship is raised from the bottom of the bay and that your people are given the chance to rest in peace."

The captain eyed me suspiciously. "You would do that for us? Why, if we're not responsible for your troublesome fog?"

"Because it's the right thing to do," I said.

"And since when do your kind concern themselves with the right thing?" the captain asked.

"My kind?" I repeated.

"You know," the captain said. His voice dropped to a whisper. "The kind of supernatural on a first name basis with the gods of the underworld."

"First, you don't need to whisper. We're on a boat in the bay with no one around. Second, you're a ghost."

"What's third?" Hansen asked. "Shouldn't something be third?"

"I was just getting to that," I said, trying not to get irritated. "Third, I don't know anyone in the underworld—except my dog, and she doesn't live there anymore."

"I love dogs," Hansen said, bursting into a toothless smile.

"I'm the protector of this town," I said. "You're arguably part of my territory." I cut a quick glance at Agent Redmond for confirmation.

"Arguably," he said.

"So if I deem it appropriate to find a way to release you from your earthbound prison, then that's what will happen," I said.

The captain inclined his head. "You give us your word?"

"As an agent of the Federal Bureau of Magic, I do."

"Agent Fury," Agent Redmond said.

Out of the corner of my eye, I noticed John begin to stir. Time to move.

"Thank you for your candor," I said to the spirits. I conjured a blast of air to scatter the salt circle, causing the shades to evaporate. I collected the rune rocks in a rush and dumped them into my handbag before John's eyes opened.

"Did I take a nap?" John stretched his arms over his head.

"Just a short one," I said. "You seemed sleepy so I didn't disturb you."

141

"I swear it's this fog," he said. "Did you find what you were looking for?"

I retrieved the fragment of the ship from the deck and tucked it into my handbag. "I did, thanks so much."

"Oh, man. I'm sorry I missed it."

"There'll be more to see soon enough," I said. "Now that we've located the ship, we can make arrangements to raise it from the water."

John clapped Agent Redmond on the back. "A worthwhile trip for you then."

Agent Redmond offered a stiff smile. "Apparently."

"If you wouldn't mind heading back to shore, John, I have a few things I need to do." In reality, I had no idea what I needed to do. Now that I knew the victims on the Brizo weren't responsible for the fog, I was back at square one.

John crossed the deck. "Man, I sure hope this fog lifts soon. It's made fishing impossible and you know how much I like to fish."

"Hopefully, everything will get back to normal," I said. And if Manfred's death was any indication, normal couldn't come soon enough.

CHAPTER FIFTEEN

I MANAGED to ditch Agent Redmond at the waterfront and drove straight home to unload my bag and wash off the salty stench of fish and dead mariners. I'd just finished drying my face when my phone rang. No rest for the wicked, apparently.

"What's up, Neville?"

"There's been another incident," he said. "You're needed quickly."

My pulse sped up. "Where?"

"Manchego Circle. Number three."

"Did you tell Agent Redmond?"

"No, he isn't here," Neville said.

"Good. Let's keep it that way." I didn't need him breathing down my neck while I tried to work. I tucked away my phone and grabbed my handbag from the counter.

Five minutes later, I arrived at the scene. Thanks to the fog, it wasn't until I pulled into the driveway and opened the car door that I saw the reason for the call.

A body was impaled on the post of a white picket fence. A

woman stood beside the body and I realized she was holding his hand.

"Great balls of fury," I breathed. I forced myself closer for a better view. The body was dressed in dark trousers and a matching suit jacket.

"Are you Agent Fury?" the woman asked.

I pulled myself together. "I am. Can you tell me what happened?"

She inclined her head toward the body. "I think it's obvious."

My throat became dry. "Right, but a little detail would be helpful. Who is he?"

"Oh, of course." She squeezed her eyes closed and gave an agitated shake of her head. "I'm sorry. I'm not thinking straight. It's a wonder I had the wherewithal to call your office instead of the police."

I leaned forward to inspect the body and noticed the fangs in his slightly open mouth. "Vampire," I said softly.

She nodded. "His name is Henry Maitland. I'm his girl-friend, Lizette."

I didn't see any fangs in her mouth. "You're a…?"

"A muse," Lizette said. "Henry and I met on a supernatural dating site. I moved here last year to be with him." Her brows knitted together. "I never thought it would end like this."

"Now that I'm here, you should call the police before a neighbor does," I said.

"We're shrouded in fog," Lizette said. "I figured that would buy us time. I did scream, though, when I saw him. Someone might have heard me."

A lump formed in my throat. "You *saw* him?"

She nodded and pointed to a tree that towered over their front yard. "He jumped from that branch."

"Oh, Lizette. I'm so sorry."

A tear slid down her cheek. "I've been trying to keep it together until you got here." She squeezed his hand. "I didn't want to leave him alone."

"Any idea why he would stake himself?" I asked.

She let out an almost imperceptible sigh. "He'd been down this week. More down than usual. He was prone to angst." She managed a smile. "Typical vampire. I'd sworn off them after my last boyfriend. He was so full of existential dread, I couldn't take it anymore."

"But you fell for Henry anyway?"

She glanced at him. "I did. He was so kind and compassionate. We started talking online and I couldn't wait to meet him. The moment we did, I knew I wanted to be with him for the rest of my life."

"Did you have any idea that he was contemplating suicide?" I asked.

"Not really. Like I said, he seemed more subdued than normal. He asked for his sausages to be extra bloody this morning, but that's about it in terms of deviation from his routine."

"He's wearing a suit," I said.

"He wears one to work every day," Lizette said. "I always choose his tie." She reached over and stroked the red tie around his neck. "I picked this one this morning. Red's his favorite color." More tears began to flow.

I glanced up at the tree. "You're certain he jumped?"

"Yes." Her voice was nearly inaudible.

"Okay. You should call the police and report it now. Are you ready?"

She bit her lip and nodded. "I just tell him everything I told you, minus the supernatural details, right?"

I patted her arm. "Yes. Don't worry. You'll do great."

"Would you stay with Henry while I call?" Lizette asked.

"I need to go inside. I left my phone on the bottom step after I called you. I know it's silly, but I hate to leave him alone."

"Of course, but I'm going to leave before the chief gets here," I said. I didn't want to make him suspicious of me. There was no obvious reason for me to be here.

Lizette reluctantly let go of Henry's hand and retreated into the house. I stood, enveloped by the fog, and waited for her to return. It was difficult to look at Henry. He seemed so peaceful and yet he'd obviously been a tortured individual. To a certain degree, I understood and empathized with his angst. It wasn't easy to be a supernatural in this world. Hiding our true natures took a toll on some of us. Fighting our true natures was an added toll. A vampire like Henry likely battled his inner demon —the one that craved blood and urged him to bite. The instinct wasn't strong in every vampire; Sally didn't seem to struggle in this world and she arrived here later in life from Otherworld, though I suspected her OCD tendencies were connected to her inability to fully embrace her true nature.

A familiar car cut through the fog and came to a stop on the shoulder of the road. Clara emerged with her purse slung over her shoulder. Her brow lifted when she spotted me.

"One of yours?"

I nodded.

Her gaze flickered to Henry's body. "Wow. I wasn't expecting that."

"What are you doing here?" I asked.

Clara gestured to the house next door. "A neighbor called to report a commotion. She heard a scream and then nothing, but was too afraid to leave the house and check it out. Cal sent me to see whether it's newsworthy." She pursed her lips at the sight of the staked vampire. "I guess it is."

"What about Gasper?" I asked. Gasper Cawdrey generally received the juicier assignments for the local newspaper.

"He's behaving strangely," Clara said. "Cal didn't even bother to call him."

I frowned. "How so?"

She shrugged. "Won't leave his house. Won't answer his phone either. Cal had to go over and check on him yesterday to make sure he was alive."

"What's wrong with him? Is he sick?"

"No, he was fine. Just said he doesn't feel like dealing with anyone right now. Wants his space. According to Cal, he was playing video games and eating junk food."

"That is strange. You'd think he'd be all over any story that came in right now."

"He may not be, but I am. I see it as a golden opportunity," Clara said. She looked at Henry. "Was it murder?"

"Suicide," I said.

Clara contemplated the body. "A vampire staked himself on a white picket fence? If this isn't a commentary on the American dream, I don't know what is."

"His girlfriend saw him jump, but she was too late to stop him."

Clara whistled. "First Manfred Rice and now this guy?"

"His name's Henry Maitland," I said. "Lizette went inside to call the police. She's obviously pretty shaken up."

"Do you mind if I talk to her?" Clara asked.

"That's up to you. It isn't my goal to interfere with news reporting unless it directly impacts supernaturals."

Clara cast a nervous glance around the neighborhood. "I know. I guess that's why I asked. I don't want to shine a spotlight somewhere it doesn't need to be. On the other hand, I'm tired of all the minor news I have to cover. It would be nice to write about a more significant event." Her cheeks colored. "Wow. That sounds horrible."

"No, it doesn't," I said. "Henry's death is significant. I'm sure his girlfriend would appreciate talking about him. Maybe it'll be cathartic for her."

"At this point, I'm desperate to stay out of the office so I don't have to field the petty phone calls."

"What do you mean?"

Clara blew a stray hair from her eye. "We've been inundated with calls from residents complaining about the most random stuff, like people driving too fast through the neighborhood, people blowing fog horns, public urination…"

"Why are they calling the newspaper to report this?" I asked. "Why not the police?"

"Apparently they *are* calling the police, but Sean and Chief Fox can't handle all the smaller inquiries, so the callers are looking for immediate gratification elsewhere."

My nose wrinkled. "Where's the public urination happening?" So I could avoid the area.

"A few places," Clara said. "This fog is making people act out."

I glanced at the body on the post. "Or just act."

Clara sighed. "This fog must've felt like a black cloud of depression all around him."

"You minored in psychology in college," I said. "Do you think the prolonged fog could trigger suicidal thoughts?" If that was the case, then Manfred and Henry might have jumped of their own volition, which would mean that there was nothing supernatural about the situation at all.

Clara cocked her head, thinking. "Depression often has its victims feeling trapped in their lives. It's possible that the fog rolled in and exacerbated it."

"To the point of suicide, though?" I asked.

Clara waved a hand through the gray mist. "Think about how you feel when you don't get enough natural sunlight."

I thought of the sun lamp in my office. "Very crabby," I said.

"And you're a typical person." Clara stopped. "Well, not really, but you know what I mean. You're not prone to depression or anxiety."

"Have you been in touch with the local suicide hotline? It wouldn't surprise me to learn they've been receiving more calls than usual."

Clara's eyes widened. "That's a good idea. Maybe I can use this as a chance to build awareness and make sure anyone feeling trapped gets help, especially while we're still blanketed in fog."

"I'm sure Henry's girlfriend would like that angle," I said. "Use his death as a springboard to help others."

"Manfred, too," Clara said.

"Absolutely."

Clara gave me a quick hug. "I love this idea. Thanks, Eden."

"I didn't do anything." I glanced over my shoulder at Henry's house. "I'm a little worried, though. If this fog doesn't lift soon, we could have complete chaos on our hands."

"Not to mention a town that stinks of pee," Clara added.

I cringed. "Thanks for that."

Lizette opened the front door with the phone in her hand. "He's on the way," she called.

I turned back to Clara. "I need to go before the police get here. Good luck. Let me know if you learn anything noteworthy."

"Thanks," Clara said. "Same to you."

With a final glance at Henry's lifeless body, I hurried to my car, a hundred thoughts whirring in my mind. The fog seemed no closer to lifting. We needed something other than luck right now. We needed divine intervention, or, at the very least, Mother Nature's intervention.

. . .

I drove to the office to update Neville on Henry Maitland. Agent Redmond was still MIA. Maybe I'd get lucky and the trip on John's boat had made him seasick. For the next few days.

"If the murdered spirits of the Brizo aren't to blame, then what is?" Neville asked.

I spun around in my chair. "I wish I knew." At least Sidrach Seaman was getting a nice vacation out of it. Maybe he'd be less grumpy upon his return.

"It's unfortunate that Agent Redmond arrived when he did," Neville said. "You have enough to worry about without the added stress of the FBM's presence."

"I agree." I tapped my pen on the desk. "The last thing I want to think about is personality tests and or doing the lift."

Neville inclined his head. "The lift?"

I flicked a dismissive finger. "From *Dirty Dancing*. It's a metaphor. Sort of."

"At least he seems to be less focused on your training than he was initially," Neville said. "It allows you a little breathing room to work."

I frowned at my computer screen. "He is less focused now, isn't he?" I paused, thinking. "It's odd."

Neville rubbed his chin. "Well, he does appear quite smitten with Clara, not that I blame him. She's fetching."

"It isn't just to do with Clara, though," I said. "When we were on the boat, he knocked magic dust out of my hand. I thought it was an accident, but what if he did it to try to ruin the summoning?"

"Why would he want that?"

"So that I wouldn't discover that the ghosts had nothing to do with the fog. To keep the spotlight from moving on to someone else." My heart began to beat faster. "Like we said, the fog's appearance coincides with his arrival. What if it isn't a coincidence?"

The wizard's eyes rounded. "You suspect Agent Redmond of creating this fog? Of driving people to their deaths? For what purpose?"

I hesitated. "I don't really know yet." A thought occurred to me. "What if he's not who he says he is?"

"Then he would have us all fooled," Neville said.

"And Clara would be in danger," I said. I didn't like that one bit. "You're handy with computers. Can you hack the FBM system?"

Neville began to choke. "You want me to what?"

"Is that hard?"

He coughed and sputtered until I handed him a bottle of water and he took a desperate drink. "It's the Federal Bureau of Magic. Of course it's hard."

"Oh. I thought you were a wizard with real computer skills," I said. "Sorry, my mistake."

Neville hurried over to my desk. "Hold on. I didn't say I couldn't do it. Just that it would be difficult."

I suppressed a smile and rolled my seat to the side to make room for Neville. "I'll leave you to it then."

His fingers flew fast and furiously over the keyboard.

"Are you using magic?" I asked.

He cast me a sidelong glance. "No, Agent Fury. I'm using typing skills."

"Oh." I watched the screen as different screens opened. I recognized the FBM logo. Finally, Agent Redmond's image appeared. "Quinn Redmond, there he is."

We read the information together. Nothing seemed to suggest Agent Redmond was our culprit.

"Well, obviously his agenda would be hidden," Neville said. "It's not as though you would expect it to be spelled out in an FBM file."

I forced a laugh. "Of course not. That would be silly." But, truth be told, I was kind of hoping it would be. "We can try a spell."

Neville stopped typing. "On a federal agent?"

"Bad idea, huh? What else can we do, though?"

The wizard ran his thumb back and forth over the mouse, contemplating our options.

"Please stop that," I said.

He looked at me. "Stop what?"

I tapped his hand. "The thumb. Can you keep it still?"

"You need my thumb to be still?"

"It's bugging me," I said. "I don't like the movement."

Neville's brow furrowed. "Is it a fury thing?"

"Yes," I lied. "Yes, it is."

His thumb stopped moving and I relaxed. "What kind of spell do you propose?" he asked. "A truth potion of some sort?"

"Those aren't foolproof," I said. "I'm thinking one that reveals his true nature, or at least his true intentions."

Neville's thumb began to move again and I fixed him with a hard stare. The thumb stopped.

"I hate to say it," Neville began, "but you know who the best resource would be for a spell like that?"

I squeezed my eyes closed. "Please don't say it. I don't want to ask for their help." Certainly not for official FBM business.

"But they'd be much more capable than I would," Neville said.

I opened my eyes to look at him. "And your hands would remain clean if we got caught," I said. "How convenient."

His mouth split in a proud grin. "Well, there is that aspect."

"Fair enough, Neville. Plausible deniability. I get it." I squared my shoulders. "For Clara's sake, I will ask for their help." In the meantime, I'd have to keep her and Agent Redmond apart until I knew what the situation was. If he was responsible for recent events in Chipping Cheddar, then the fae was far more dangerous than he appeared.

CHAPTER SIXTEEN

My mother stood at the island with a bag of potato chips, crunching happily.

"You're eating chips?" I asked. My mother was generally far too vain to gobble down junk food. She knew the impact it had on skin and never let an opportunity slip by to remind me.

My mother curled the top of the bag closed. "So what?"

"No reason." I didn't need to get zapped with a zit on my nose for saying the wrong thing. "Where's Grandma?"

"Why would you want to know that? It's not like you two are on the best terms."

I examined her closely. My mother usually had no problem inviting conflict. Hiding Grandma's whereabouts only meant one thing.

"What have you done?"

She raised her chin a fraction. "Nothing she didn't deserve."

Uh oh. "Whatever you did, can you bring her back?"

"Why would you want me to do that? You don't even like Grandma." She stashed the potato chip bag in the pantry and

154

returned to her crossword puzzle on the island. "What's a five letter word for making amends?"

"If I tell you, will you bring back Grandma from whatever hell she's in?"

My mother pursed her lips. "Fine, but you'd better protect me from the consequences."

"You two can work out your own issues," I said. "I've got my own situation with Grandma at the moment."

"You really should've left her burnbook alone."

My jaw clenched. "Atone is the word you're looking for."

She lit up. "Yes, I think it is." She scribbled down the letters and set down her pen. "Now, let me see what I can do about Grandma."

"I need Aunt Thora, too," I said. "The family coven."

She raised an eyebrow. "I see. Well, you've certainly piqued my curiosity."

"Not really my goal, but whatever. So where's Aunt Thora? I'll get her while you...reinstate Grandma."

My mother ran her tongue over her upper lip. "You'll have to figure that one out for yourself."

"Are you serious? You hexed them both? Why?"

She pushed aside her crossword puzzle. "Because I was trying to do my puzzle in peace and quiet and those two wouldn't stop nattering on about Mrs. Paulson's lawn service coming too early in the morning. I couldn't take it anymore."

"You hexed them for talking too much?" That seemed extreme, even for my family.

"I told you, I couldn't concentrate."

I prayed to the gods for sanity. "Where's Aunt Thora?"

"Check the garden," she mumbled.

"The garden? Is she a gnome? A toadstool?" The possibilities were endless.

My mother smoothed the back of her hair. "A lemon."

I buried my face in my hands. "You turned your aunt into a lemon on one of her own lemon trees?"

"She was being sour," my mother said. "The punishment fit the crime."

"And what about Grandma?" I asked. If Aunt Thora was a lemon, I could only imagine what had been done to Grandma.

Before she could answer, Charlemagne slithered through the kitchen clutching a toy in his strong jaws. Princess Buttercup bounded after the python and tried to steal away the raggedy doll. The playful game of tug-of-war quickly turned violent as Princess Buttercup snatched the toy and Charlemagne hissed noisily. The hellhound responded with a guttural growl that made the hair on the back of my neck stand on end.

"That's enough, you two," I said firmly. I swiped the doll from Princess Buttercup and grimaced as my fingers touched a layer of slime. "You two need to learn to play nicely or not at all." I turned back to my mother. "Now, where's Grandma?"

My mother smirked. "I do believe you're holding her now."

I stared at the bitten raggedy doll in my hand. "You turned her into a chew toy?"

"I turned her into an inanimate object so she'd shut up," my mother said. "I can't help it if Candy swished her tail and knocked the doll onto the floor where Charlemagne found it."

I groaned. "She could be hurt. She's an old woman."

My mother narrowed her eyes. "She's fine and you know it. That witch can withstand Armageddon with one hand tied behind her back."

My mother wasn't wrong. I held open my sticky palm. "Turn her back. Now."

She scraped back her chair and took the doll from my outstretched hand. "I'll deal with Grandma. You get Aunt Thora."

Part of me wanted to wait and see how Grandma responded to being turned into fodder for pythons, but I decided not to dawdle.

I exited the back door and traipsed across the lawn until I reached Aunt Thora's lemon orchard. Okay, a few trees probably didn't qualify as an orchard, but this was her special patch of land and she grew her favorite fruit on it.

I planted my feet in front of the first tree and scrutinized the yellow fruit. Which one was Aunt Thora? I touched one of the larger lemons, but nothing about it seemed magical. I moved on to the next tree and stopped short when I noticed a lemon with what appeared to be pale freckles. Aunt Thora's pale freckles.

I plucked the lemon from the branch and returned with it to the kitchen, where my mom and Grandma were locked in a battle of wills. Grandma's hair was slick with film from the animals and her clothes were torn.

I held up the lemon for inspection. "This lemon has freckles."

Grandma grabbed the lemon from me. "I'll take care of this." She stalked out of the room.

I faced my mother. "You're going to pay for that one."

My mother seemed satisfied with her evil deed. "The fur babies enjoyed it."

"I don't think Charlemagne counts as a fur baby. He has snakeskin."

Grandma and Aunt Thora returned to the kitchen, slightly subdued. Grandma had used a spell to fix her appearance. Neither one would look at my mother.

"If it's any consolation," I told Aunt Thora, "your scent is amazing."

Aunt Thora sniffed under her arms. "It is, isn't it?"

My mother joined us at the island. "Okay, sweetheart. We're all assembled. What is it that you need from Team Evil?"

Now that the moment of truth was here, I found my will dissolving. I loathed asking for their help. It was against all my principles. I forced myself to think of Manfred Rice and Henry Maitland. I had to know whether Agent Redmond was responsible.

"I need help with a spell." My voice was so low, I doubted anyone heard me.

"You want what?" My mother's eyes popped with such force that I was worried her eyeballs would drop out.

"I want your help with a spell," I mumbled.

Her lips curved into a satisfied smile. "Louder, please, sweetheart. I couldn't quite hear you."

"She wants help with a spell," Grandma shouted. "Great Goddess, I'm eighty-six and I heard her. Clean out your ears."

"I have to make sure that Agent Redmond has nothing to do with the fog."

"Why do you need us for that?' Aunt Thora asked. "You can do that kind of magic without help."

My mother gave her a knowing smile. "Eden doesn't want her training instructor to know what she's up to. She needs the kind of spell he won't detect."

Joy radiated from Grandma. "Which means she needs dark magic."

"It's not a particularly powerful spell, Eden," my mother said. "You wouldn't need all of us."

"Good, because I'm not helping," Grandma said.

"Why not?" Aunt Thora asked.

Grandma glowered at me. "She knows why."

"The burnbook," I said.

Aunt Thora held up her index finger. "I can do it in potion form. Make it taste like butterscotch."

"Traitor," Grandma hissed.

"It wasn't my burnbook," Aunt Thora said. "How quickly do you need this?"

"I'm going to arrange to meet he and Clara at The Cheese Wheel tonight," I said. "I'd like to make sure I get this potion into him at the bar."

"The Cheese Wheel is open for business?" my mother asked. "I heard Chief Fox was instituting a curfew that restricted business hours."

"They're allowed to stay open until ten," I said. "I'm sure the restrictions are hurting businesses, though."

"The whole town is hurting because of this ridiculous fog," Grandma complained. "If that fairy man is responsible, I may take matters into my own hands."

My jaw clenched. "You will not. I am handling this."

"Not very well," Grandma shot back. "How many more have to die before you figure out what's happening?"

I was tempted to turn my grandmother back into the chew toy, but restrained myself. I needed the potion more than I needed petty revenge.

"Do you really think Agent Redmond has something to do with the fog?" my mother asked. "He seems far too handsome."

I ignored her.

"Your mother and I will work on your potion now," Aunt Thora said.

"That'll be a hundred dollars," my mother said. "I'll write you a receipt and you can submit it with your expenses."

"Mom! I can't expense it. Then they'll know I used black magic on an FBM agent."

My mother shrugged. "Then I guess you're out a hundred dollars, sweetheart. Good news is you live here rent free."

"Even if Legolas is responsible," Grandma said, "what's his end game? Does he have some ancient grudge against Chipping Cheddar?"

"I have no idea," I said, "but that's exactly what I intend to find out."

The Cheese Wheel was even more crowded than karaoke night. Clara, Agent Redmond, and I stood in a tight circle. I bopped my head to the music, waiting for my moment to strike. I hoped that simply administering the black magic potion didn't trigger a new fury power.

I slipped my hand into my pocket and wrapped my fingers around the tiny vial. I couldn't let anyone see me. Clara would realize I was up to something if she saw me with a potion. I wasn't like my mother, who carried as many potions in her handbag as lipsticks.

"Let's order shots," I said, loud enough to be heard over the music.

"Shots?" Agent Redmond repeated. "I haven't had shots since…well, never."

Why didn't that surprise me? "It wouldn't hurt you to loosen up. You're not on duty now."

"True." Agent Redmond relented far more quickly than I expected. "Would you like one, Clara?"

"I'll get the first round." I made a beeline for the counter before anyone could object. I made sure my back was to them when I ordered so they couldn't see what I was up to. I ordered three different shots and quickly dumped the contents of the vial into Agent Redmond's glass. Normally, he'd be trained to detect any kind of magic in his food or drink, but my family's brand of magic was too slick and powerful to be identified using typical FBM procedures. They could slip a spell past an average agent without much trouble.

I slipped the empty vial back in my pocket and turned around with a shot glass in each hand. "A toast," I said. "Here, Agent Redmond. A glass for you." I handed him the shot glass filled with the potion.

He sniffed the liquid once before downing it. "Butterscotch," he said, smacking his lips.

Clara drank hers and licked her lips. "Mine was more like peppermint."

"Because I know that's your favorite," I said quickly. I watched Agent Redmond closely to see whether he noticed a potion mixed in with the liquor, but he seemed oblivious.

"Where's yours, Eden?" Clara asked.

I swiped mine from the counter. "Mine's called a Foggy Bottom," I said. "I figured I'd go with a theme."

Agent Redmond laughed. "I like it."

I downed the alcohol and welcomed the warmth in the pit of my stomach. I was glad I ate dinner before I came. Too many drinks on an empty stomach and I'd end up dancing on top of the bar wearing only my badge. I knew this from an unfortunate experience that I'd almost successfully blocked from memory.

I continued to observe Agent Redmond for signs that the potion was taking effect. I pulled out my phone. "Who wants me to play a song on the jukebox?" I selected Cyndi Lauper's *True Colors* to set the mood.

"A slow song?" Clara asked. "That kind of brings the mood down, don't you think?"

"It's like when your mother comes home early from work and you're upstairs with your girlfriend," Agent Redmond said. "Buzzkill."

I gaped at Agent Redmond. "Okay then."

"We should get a bottle of champagne before the bar closes," Clara said. "We can bring it back to my place."

"Great idea," Agent Redmond said, smiling at her. "You're so smart, Clara. And beautiful. And funny."

Okay, that was enough of that. I couldn't have him reeling her in with compliments if he was going to turn out to be the bad guy. Time to test the potion.

I snapped my fingers in front of his face. "Agent Redmond, what are your intentions here?"

He blinked at me. "My true intentions are to take Clara to her house, kiss her senseless, and then steal her underpants to wear later as a trophy." Agent Redmond's hand slapped against his mouth. "Why did I say that?"

I wore a look of shock. "I have no idea. I was only joking."

Clara scrunched her nose. "You want to steal my underpants?"

Agent Redmond faltered. "I…Well. What color are they?"

"Purple."

He seemed to contemplate her answer. "Bikini, thong, or briefs?"

"Boy shorts," she replied.

Agent Redmond shuddered with pleasure. "I hadn't even considered boy shorts."

This was not the direction I expected the conversation to take.

"Any other intentions?" I asked.

Agent Redmond glanced at Clara. "To see her again once my assignment here is over. I travel frequently, as you can imagine, but I'd come back whenever possible to see her."

"I'd love to see you, too," Clara gushed.

Huh. "Even with the underwear fetish?" I asked.

Clara's adoring gaze was pinned on Agent Redmond. "It's not really that strange when you think about it. It's a way of feeling close to me when I'm not with him. Isn't that right, Quinn?"

He snaked an arm around her waist. "Yes, plus I like the way the fabric feels against my skin."

Well, that settled it. Agent Redmond had nothing to do with the fog. There was no way he'd confess to an underwear fetish unless the potion had worked. I was both disappointed and relieved.

"Why did you knock the jar out of my hand on the boat?" I asked.

"Are you still upset about that?" he said. "It was an accident, Agent Fury. The boat rocked and I wanted to keep you from falling."

So it really had been an accident.

"You need another shot, Eden," Clara said.

"We all do," Agent Redmond said. "I feel like celebrating."

"Why?" I asked. "We still have fog and I haven't finished my training."

"You should be more optimistic, Agent Fury. It's not all gloom and doom in this world." He stepped up to the counter. "Three more shots, please." He took a glass off the counter and gave it to me. "Foggy Bottoms up!"

I gulped down the sweet liquid and felt the comfortable burn in my stomach.

"Was it good?" Clara asked.

"It's delicious."

Agent Redmond and Clara finished their shots.

"Here you are!" Sassy's loud voice cut through the buzz of the bar. "We made it before curfew."

My stomach turned over when I saw that Tanner was with her. So much for any chance of an elevated mood.

"Look at this," Tanner said smoothly. "Now there's a sandwich I wouldn't mind being in the middle of."

Sassy elbowed him in the ribs. "He's already had a few beers at the house," she said, by way of apology.

Tanner looked around the bar. "Business is booming. The

chief won't really shut down the place early, will he?"

Sassy strained to listen to the music. "Why are they playing such dull music? We need something more up-tempo." She whipped out her phone and went to the music app, immediately changing the song.

"How did you do that?" I asked.

"I just paid more," Sassy said. "You can stop any song in the middle if you're willing to pay."

"Seems unfair," I said.

"Says the girl with magic," Clara started and then stopped. "Magical money." She laughed and hiccupped.

"Your money is magic, huh?" Tanner winked at me. "If I'd known that, I might have made different choices."

I never wanted to kick someone so hard in the pants, not even suspects I was trying to apprehend.

Tanner glanced over my head and groaned. "I guess he's serious about the curfew if he's come to enforce it himself."

I whirled around to see Chief Fox swagger into the bar in uniform. Our eyes locked and I felt a jolt of electricity. I forgot all about Agent Redmond, Tanner, the fog—anything that wasn't Sawyer Fox. Right now, I wanted nothing more than to run through the bar and throw myself into his arms.

"Eden, are you okay?" Clara touched my arm and quickly jerked away. "Wow. Too much."

I managed to avert my gaze and Chief Fox did the same. He went to the counter to talk to the bartender, probably to tell him to stop serving.

"I need the bathroom," I said. I pushed my way through the crowd only to find a long line for the women's restroom. Naturally, the men's room was empty, so I decided to zip in there before anyone beat me to it. I didn't want to become a public urination statistic.

I peed quickly and washed my hands. When I opened the door to exit, I was greeted with a familiar chest.

"Chief Fox," I said. My eyes traveled up to the dimple in his chin and the rest of his sexy face.

"You realize this is the wrong room for you," he said.

I looked around me and feigned surprise. "I was wondering how that urinal got there. They should really make these bathrooms unisex."

He took a step forward, forcing me back into the restroom. "While we have a moment alone, there's something I've been meaning to tell you."

My heartbeat was thundered in my ears. "Oh?"

He managed to close the door behind him without turning around. "I've been wanting to thank you."

"Thank me? Why?" I asked. He was standing so close that my fingers started to itch to touch his hair. To touch him anywhere really.

"The idea for taking dogs on patrol," he said. "That came from you."

I licked my lips. "I thought you said you read an article."

His mouth split in a grin. "I lied. The inspiration came from you. When you told me how you rescued Princess Buttercup, I remembered thinking how awesome that was. She's a great dog."

"She is." I frowned. "So you decided to help other rescue dogs get adopted?"

"I'm out in the community every day. Why not provide two services at once? These dogs deserve a second chance at life."

"I totally agree."

"The first dog I took out was a Pit Bull mix," he said. "His reputation preceded him, you know? So it was hard getting people interested, according to the shelter."

"Pit Bulls are the ones that are supposed to be aggressive?"

"Yeah, the general consensus seems to be they're inher-

165

ently vicious and evil, but it's no different from people. You need to decide based on the merits of the individual dog and not the breed."

My lips parted in an effort to respond, but I was speechless. I'd never wanted to kiss anyone more in my life. Never mind the smell of bleach and urine.

Chief Fox noticed my silence. "Did I say something wrong?"

I shifted onto my toes and planted a firm kiss on his lips. "Thank you."

The chief's sea-green eyes widened. "You feel that strongly about Pit Bulls, huh?"

My cheeks burned. "I'm sorry. I don't know what came over me."

We stared at each other for a beat. The next thing I knew, his arm was around my waist and his lips were back on mine. I ended up with my back against the wall, kissing him with abandon. His fingers threaded through my hair and I lost all sense of time and place.

When we finally broke apart, my breathing was ragged and my heart felt ready to break free of my chest.

Double-decker crap sandwich. What had gotten into me? Into him?

"I shouldn't have done that," I said. My voice was barely above a whisper.

The chief seemed equally stunned by his own behavior. "I guess we're really passionate about dogs."

Someone knocked on the door. "Hurry up in there!"

"Stay behind me and they won't see you," the chief whispered. He turned and opened the door. "Time to go home, everyone."

People began to boo. I used the distraction as an opportunity to slip out from behind him and escape the bar—as well as my feelings.

CHAPTER SEVENTEEN

THE NEXT MORNING, I opened the back door to my father's house and attempted to enter the kitchen. I hoped to talk to my father about the debunked theories and do a little brainstorming. As a vengeance demon, I figured he might have insight into other possibilities.

Sally stood in the middle of the white tile floor with a mop in her hand and a bucket of water beside her. She threw up a hand when she saw me.

"Not one step more, Eden Fury. You'll leave tracks."

My foot hovered over the tile. "I can't come in?"

"Only if you use your wings and fly over to the living room," she replied, completely serious.

"You know I only use my wings for emergencies." Sally knew I was uncomfortable with my fury powers and endeavored not to use them, certainly not to avoid walking on a wet tile floor.

"Sally, you're being OTT," my father said. Although I couldn't see him, I could hear his booming voice emanating from the living room. "That means over the top, Eden."

"Thanks," I called. "I'm familiar with the term."

167

"Go around to the front door," Sally said. "You can come in that way."

I didn't argue. This was Sally's house as much as my father's. If she didn't want my wet footprints on her kitchen floor, then so be it.

I trudged around the house and entered via the front door as requested. My father stood in the living room with the vacuum.

"Wait. You're cleaning, too?" I asked, incredulous. My father was known for wreaking vengeance on people, not germs.

He made a disgruntled face. "Your stepmom is on a tear."

"Clearly." I peered around the corner into the kitchen where Sally was attacking the floor with the mop. "Is she upset about something?" Her OCD tended to flare when she was angry or upset. When I was younger, I always knew when they'd been fighting because their house sparkled like an unblemished diamond.

"I think she's fed up with the fog," he said.

"Aren't we all?"

"She doesn't like to drive when visibility is low, so she's taking out her frustration on the house." He paused. "And me."

"She shouldn't be driving anyway," I said. "Chief Fox has encouraged everyone to stay home as much as possible in the interest of public safety. There've been too many accidents."

"Yeah, yeah." My father unplugged the vacuum. "Watch where you step. If you leave impressions in the carpet, she'll make me do it again."

"I'd offer for you to seek refuge at our house, but I know you won't."

My father barked a short laugh. "When hell freezes over."

"Hey, with this fog, you never know."

Sally poked her head over the counter. "Can I get you a drink or a snack, Eden?"

"Please say no," my father said under his breath. "She'll spend an hour cleaning up afterward."

"No, thanks," I said. It was hard to resist Sally's baked goods, but I didn't want to annoy my dad.

"I heard your mother killed your grandmother the other day." My father couldn't resist a smile. "I have to admit I kind of miss those days."

"Everyone's tempers have been flaring lately," I said. "My gut tells me it's connected to the fog, but I can't put my fingers on it."

"This fog is driving me to distraction," my father said. "I haven't been able to get on the golf course in over a week. I've got no outlet for my frustrations."

"Unlike Sally," I said, nodding toward the kitchen where the manic vampire was now polishing the handles on the cabinets.

"She's been building up to this," my father said. "It started a few days ago with dusting the blinds and escalated from there."

"Sorry," I said. It couldn't be easy for either one of them.

"Rafael called me yesterday to give me an earful about the werewolves," my father said. "I mean, I love Julie and Meg, but what a bunch of nuts the rest of them are. Did you know Hugh ordered a mail order bride?"

"He mentioned it. He said that pack numbers are low and they don't want to interbreed."

"You'd have to go much further south for that," my father said. "Apparently, the fog has delayed the delivery of his bride and he was throwing a fit outside the post office."

I stiffened. "What kind of fit?"

"Don't bend your badge. He didn't shift right there. He waited until he reached the woods."

"In broad daylight?" I asked.

"He's not the only one. Rafael said a bunch of werewolves have stopped taking their blockers so they can shift. Not Meg and Julie, of course." My father patted my arm. "Rafael told me what happened with Meg, by the way. It was good of you to get involved."

"Meg's was an isolated incident," I said. "She didn't intend to steal. She only acted on impulse…" I stopped talking.

"What's the matter?" my father asked.

"Impulse," I said. "That's the common factor in everyone's behavior." Including mine in the men's room with Chief Fox. My cheeks grew flushed remembering the heated moment.

"Sure, Sally has control issues, but I don't see how everyone could be suffering from the same disorder all of the sudden."

"It's the fog."

"The fog is a disorder?" my father asked.

I shot to my feet. "I need to get to the office."

"Watch where you step," Sally called from the kitchen. "Take off your shoes on the way out."

My father rolled his eyes. "If this fog doesn't disappear soon, then I'm going to."

"I can't believe I didn't put it all together before," I said. I sat in my office across the table from Neville and Agent Redmond, sharing my new theory.

Neville shook his head. "An impetus demon makes so much sense." He cast a glance at Agent Redmond. "Impetus is Latin for impulse."

"I'm familiar with Latin, thank you," Agent Redmond said. The fae raked a hand through his perfect hair. "This is why I prefer training and protocol. Much easier to predict."

"Almost everyone in town has been fighting a losing

battle against their impulses," I said. I directed my attention to Agent Redmond. "You've been eating carbs and shirking responsibility in order to spend time with Clara."

He lowered his gaze. "Admittedly, my behavior has been out of character. It's been similar to an out-of-body experience."

"You're going to wish you were out of your body when you get home and weigh yourself," I said. "You've eaten a lot of donuts."

"No regrets," Agent Redmond said.

"I saw a little boy run into the road to get a ball. Werewolves are shifting in the daytime. People are stealing. My family is zapping each other for minor infractions." I drew a deep breath. "The crazy poker games. Simon losing all his money."

"That also explains Manfred Rice and Henry Maitland," Neville said. "They'd been successfully fighting suicidal impulses for years."

"Until the fog rolled in," I said. Sweet Hecate, I hated that stupid fog with a passion.

"My contacts in Madrid say that the impetus demon escaped through their portal," Agent Redmond said. "They thought it dissipated when it hit the human atmosphere, so they didn't bother to alert anyone."

"But instead it crossed an ocean to get here," I said.

"We only track reports from North American portals anyway," Neville said.

"It might be time to change the protocol," Agent Redmond suggested. "I'll raise it with headquarters."

Neville checked the screen of his phone. "Apparently, the demon can't take corporeal form. It won't be easy to defeat."

"It's always in some kind of mist form?" I asked.

"Basically," Neville replied. "Which means you can't kill it in any traditional sense."

Terrific. "Then what are the options?" I asked.

"You need magic powerful enough to disrupt it on a cellular level and then bend it to your will," Neville said. "I think have a viable plan."

I looked at him expectantly. "Go for it."

Neville rubbed his hands together. "Excellent. Do we have access to a windmill?"

I squinted at him. "A windmill?"

"Yes. You see, I've been looking at ways to eradicate fog in general and, if we match the air temperature with our own wind production, we may be able to…"

"Wait. That's your plan?" I asked. "To roll the giant windmill into the middle of town and disperse the fog over the bay?"

Neville opened his mouth, ready to offer an enthusiastic answer. He stopped and scratched his head. "I suppose it does sound ludicrous when it's said out loud."

"There's always magic," Agent Redmond said with a pointed look in my direction.

"Well, sure, if I were powerful enough to generate a tornado all by myself," I said. "But I'm not." Nor did I want that kind of power.

"Who said you had to do it by yourself?" Agent Redmond said.

I hesitated. "You want me to…?" I shook my head. "Nope. Absolutely not."

Neville glanced from Agent Redmond to me. "Oh, I see."

"Asking my family for help isn't like asking your family for help," I told Agent Redmond. "Your family probably harnesses the magic of rainbows and unicorns and then everyone joins hands and sings until your achievement's unlocked."

"It's for the greater good, Agent Fury," Agent Redmond

said. "Surely you can look past your family drama to see that."

"It isn't about my family drama," I replied. He didn't understand and I couldn't explain in detail without revealing more than I wanted to. "It's the bigger picture. First, I will owe my family big time." He had no idea what it was like to owe a favor to an evil witch. Not good, let me tell you. "Second, tapping into their magic could have negative repercussions for me personally."

"She means her fury power," Neville interjected.

"Thank you, Neville the Narrator," I said.

"What about your siphoning magic?" Agent Redmond asked. "Can you use the demon's power against it?"

"I don't think filling a fury with the power of an impulse demon is such a hot idea," I said.

Agent Redmond appeared thoughtful. "Yes, I can see how that might create more of a problem."

"It's not that I'm opposed to using magic..." I began.

"Great. Then I think the coven is our best bet," Agent Redmond said. "As a federal agent and your superior, I order you to request assistance from the local coven."

"You're ordering me?" I repeated.

"It's within the scope of my duties," Agent Redmond said. "Regulation twenty-seven, subparagraph b."

I stared at him, anger simmering just below the surface. "Fine," I said in a clipped tone. "I will do exactly as you say and request assistance from the local coven."

He folded his arms, pleased. "See? You're making progress, Agent Fury."

I flashed a plastic smile. "I'll let you know how it goes."

What Agent Redmond failed to realize was the fact that Chipping Cheddar has more than one local coven. As far as I was concerned, the LeRoux family was a better bet than mine, so I made my way to Adele's house. We served on the supernatural council together and I knew she'd be eager to offer whatever help I needed, despite our family's rivalry.

Her granddaughter Corinne answered the door, unable to disguise her shock. "Eden Fury. Come on in."

"It's good to see you, Corinne," I said.

I entered the Craftsman-Style bungalow and admired the cozy interior. It was compact but beautifully appointed with a painted white bench in the entryway and light gray walls. It was the kind of home that made guests feel comfortable, no matter who they were or why they were here.

Corinne fixed her dark eyes on me. "I find that hard to believe, but for the sake of politeness, I'll just smile and nod."

"Oh, stop," I said. "You and I have no issue with each other. Why pretend?"

"Because we represent our families," Corinne said. "My family would blow a fuse if they thought for one second I was being friendly with you."

"Well, if it's any consolation, I'm here on official FBM business."

That got her attention. "Come this way. We're all in the kitchen. Gran just made some of her homemade three-mint tea."

"Sounds delicious."

Rosalie and Adele sat at the round table in the kitchen with a pot of tea between them. Their porcelain cups were decorated with the fleur-de-lis.

"My word. Eden Fury in my home." Adele stood to greet me with a kiss on each cheek. "Normally we'd sit in the garden and have our afternoon tea, but the fog has made that unbearable."

"I don't blame you," I said. "It's unpleasant." More than she realized.

Rosalie kicked out a chair for me and I sat. She wasn't as polished as her mother or daughter, but I didn't mind her.

"What brings you to us?" Rosalie asked. "Problems at home again?" She smirked at her mother. "Remember that time Eden ran away in middle school and wanted to live with us?" She threw her head back and laughed. "Oh, boy. Your family was ready to curse us to the moon and back."

My face burned at the memory. My family had been furious, mostly because I'd chosen to seek refuge with the LeRoux family, their witchy rivals. It was the worst kind of disloyalty and they'd punished me for it. It had been one of the few times I'd been struck by lightning and they'd waited an entire day to revive me. My mother had called school and told them I had the flu. Anton had been nice to me for an entire week after I was brought back to life. I still remembered the pity in his eyes.

"Let's not dwell on the past," Adele said, sensing my distress.

"Why was it that you came here again?" Rosalie drummed her nails on the table, ignoring her mother's request. "Oh, that's right. You'd refused to add your blood to one of their spells and they'd threatened you."

"They saw it as a rite of passage," I said, weakly rising to their defense. "They didn't view it the same way I did." I hadn't wanted to acquire any fury powers by joining in the dark ritual, so I'd refused to participate. Every witch in my family had participated for centuries and I was still considered one of them, despite my mixed heritage. It had been a trying time for all of us.

"Family is a complicated beast," Corinne said. "Would you like tea, Eden?"

I gave her a grateful smile. "That would be nice, thanks."

Corinne crossed the kitchen to retrieve another cup. She poured the tea while Adele focused on me.

"I imagine you're here to tell us that the fog is mystical in nature," Adele said. "No natural fog lasts this long."

"It's an impetus demon," I said, and shared everything I'd learned so far.

"And you believe the best way to beat it is with our magic?" Adele's hand grasped at her pearl necklace.

"Apparently so," I said. I revealed more of my conversation with Agent Redmond and Neville. "Many of us have done a good job resisting our impulses, but if we don't bring an end to the fog soon, we're going to start seeing a lot more injuries and deaths."

Adele listened intently, her fingers slotted together on the table. "I hate to say it, Eden, but I think you need magic stronger than what our coven can offer you."

My heart sank. "Are you sure?"

Adele chuckled lightly. "Believe me, I'd be thrilled to step in and avoid unleashing your family's powers on this town, but we don't have the same kind of...access that you do."

I knew what she meant. The LeRoux family steered clear of black magic. It was one of the reasons I secretly liked and respected them. Well, not so much Rosalie. While I didn't mind her, I didn't actually respect her either.

"I have an idea, if you'd like to hear it," Adele continued.

"Does this idea happen to exclude me from the spell casting?" I asked. If I used powerful black magic, there was a good chance I'd gain a new fury power as a result.

"Not only do you need to participate," Adele said. "You need to act as the vessel."

My jaw unhinged.

"What do you mean?" Rosalie asked. "She needs to soak up her family's magic and spit it out?"

Adele gave a solemn nod. "More or less. Eden needs to channel their power and direct it. She's the only one who can."

I lowered my head. "Because of my siphoning power."

"That's right." Adele offered a sympathetic look. "I empathize with your reluctance, dear, and you're right to be fearful of that kind of magic. I dabbled with it as a young witch and felt its essence." She straightened in her seat. "I knew then it would never be the right fit for me."

"I didn't know you experimented," Rosalie said. "You were always stringent with me."

Adele smiled coyly. "It isn't unusual for a young witch to experiment. I was surprised you didn't do more of it."

"Now I'm wishing I had," Rosalie grumbled. "I didn't want to disappoint you."

"Same," Corinne said. "I've always walked a straight and narrow path because I wanted to be like you."

"And I'm grateful for it," Adele said. "That's the kind of coven we're meant to be."

"And why my family resents you for it," I said.

Adele sipped her tea. "The resentment runs both ways, but you already know that."

"But why?" I asked. "You don't want their kind of magic and you disapprove. Why resent them for it?"

"Because they have access to incredible power," Adele said. "Every witch wants that. We just want it without the evil strings attached."

"Do you really think the impetus demon is that strong?" I asked.

"That demon has laid siege to this town for over a week and we didn't even realize what it was," Rosalie said. "Of course it's that strong."

She had a point.

Adele patted my arm. "I'm sorry, Eden. I know you'd prefer to avoid tapping into that particular power source."

I pressed my fingers to my temples. "But for the sake of the town, I don't have much of a choice."

"You shouldn't have come back from San Francisco if you didn't want to get dragged into these messes," Rosalie said unhelpfully.

"Hush," Corinne said. "Eden didn't put herself in this position."

"I kind of did," I admitted. "If I hadn't screwed up with the FBI, I wouldn't have been sent back here."

"You can't blame yourself," Adele said. "You're here and you're doing your best. That's all that matters now."

CHAPTER EIGHTEEN

"ARE WE READY?" I asked the assembled group. We'd arrived at the vortex with a backpack full of ingredients that Neville had organized for us at my office.

My mother, Aunt Thora, Neville, and Rafael murmured their assent. Grandma hadn't turned up at the office, her act of retaliation for the burnbook.

It was almost impossible to see anything at this point. My neck hurt from straining forward to peer into the thick fog and watch for any signs of movement. The mystical energy was so strong here, though, that eyesight wasn't necessary to find it.

"Good thing the chief instituted an earlier curfew," my mother said. "He's not completely useless."

She was right. The roads were clear of other vehicles and the sliver of land between the river and the bay where the vortex was located was clear of people, which made our mission that much safer.

Neville set up the rune rocks in a circle to create a protective ward and I unzipped the backpack and set it on the

179

ground. My mother and Aunt Thora busied themselves with the herbs and candles.

"I need the bottle," I said. "Where is it?"

"Here," Neville said. He pulled it from the backpack and handed it to me as a familiar figure emerged from the fog.

"Grandma?"

"Am I wearing a glamour?" she snapped. "Of course it's me."

"I thought you didn't want to help," I said.

"You're family," she said. "Of course I want to help. Unlike some people, I'm not judgmental about the company I keep."

"You're extremely judgmental," I said.

"I'd have to agree with Eden on that one," my mother said.

Grandma rolled her eyes. "Fine, but you know what I mean."

I studied her, still wondering whether this was a trick. I wouldn't put it past her to sabotage our efforts to defeat the demon just for spite.

"You're not angry about the burnbook?" I asked.

"I was at first, but you were right," Grandma said. "I knew you'd want to find it eventually, which is why I hid it and warded it to self-destruct."

I pursed my lips. "This is the impetus demon's influence. As soon as we cast the spell, you're going to revert to type."

Grandma clucked her tongue. "You don't get it, Eden. You never have. You label us as evil…"

"Because you are," I interrupted.

"And you call us conjurers of black magic," Grandma continued.

"Because you are."

Grandma fixed me with a thousand yard stare. "But that doesn't mean we don't take care of our own, whether she wants to be a part of this family or not."

My throat constricted. "It's not that simple, Grandma."

"Exactly my point." Grandma eyed the ingredients that Neville had gathered. "Oh, good. You have hemlock. I was worried you wouldn't know to include it."

My mother studied the small white flowers on the hemlock plant. "I don't know about this one. It looks a bit sad."

"You're not choosing a corsage for the prom," Grandma said. "Just put it where it belongs."

"What are you in such a rush for?" my mother asked. "You don't even want to participate."

Grandma glanced around warily. "Let's get a move on. This conversation is creating negative energy. It'll mess up the spell."

"You breathe and it creates negative energy," I said.

Grandma batted her eyelashes. "Is that how you speak to your own grandmother? The woman who raised you when your own mother was too busy fighting with her then-husband to pay attention to her children?"

My mother's head snapped toward her. "Mom! How can you say such a thing?"

Grandma covered her mouth. "Oops, impulse control. Sorry."

"Rune rocks are sorted," Neville announced. "What's next?"

"I think the roots needs to be more finely chopped," Rafael said. "They're too chunky."

"This is why we don't include you," my mother said. "We're performing a spell, not baking a casserole."

"You don't include me because I'm a man and you hate men," Rafael said.

"That's not true," my mother said. "I love men. Ask anybody."

"It's true," Grandma said, "but don't bother to ask because they don't remember her name afterward."

Neville shifted awkwardly. "Um, could someone please light the candles now?"

Grandma patted her pockets. "Who has matches?"

"Matches?" my mother scoffed. "Use your magic."

"Use *your* magic," Grandma shot back. "I'm saving mine."

"For what—a rainy day?" my mother asked. "Get in there."

Aunt Thora let loose a shrill whistle. "That's enough, witches. It's time to stop the bickering and pull yourselves together. Now, I know as practitioners of the dark arts, we don't necessarily care about protecting people, but we do want to protect this town—if for no other reason—that we can keep living in it."

"She makes a good point," my mother said.

"Of course I do. Now, time for the blood," Aunt Thora said.

I retrieved the dagger from inside my boot and sliced my palm over the bowl. Three drops plunged into the mix, producing a puff of smoke.

Grandma eyed me cautiously. "You did that far too easily."

"She's a natural," Aunt Thora said.

I became fixated on my open wound. Grandma was right. I hadn't even hesitated. Blood trickled down my arm, but I was too immobilized to stop it.

Neville produced a handkerchief and wiped the blood away. He tucked the handkerchief into his pocket without missing a beat.

"Neville, it has my blood on it," I said.

"Nothing the laundry can't handle tomorrow," he said. "I'll stain stick it before bed."

Grandma's gaze was pinned to the bowl. "We can't go through with this." Her foot shot out to kick the bowl, but Aunt Thora cast a paralysis spell just in time. Grandma's leg hovered in mid-air.

Neville moved to stand in front of the bowl. "It's the

demon," he said. "It's trying to infiltrate us so we can't perform the spell."

"I don't want to perform this spell," I said. "It's evil."

"It's the lesser of two evils," Grandma insisted. "If we don't get rid of this demon, we can kiss this town and all of its residents goodbye. If it were just the LeRoux family, I wouldn't mind so much."

Aunt Thora grabbed my grandmother's hand. "Come on, Esther. Let's form a circle."

Rafael took my grandmother's hand. "An excellent idea. This demon is no match for our combined powers."

We stood inside the protective circle and joined hands. Aunt Thora began to chant and our voices mingled with hers.

"Nyx, Goddess of the Night, of Darkness, of Shadows, hear our plea," we said in unison.

The light of the candles flickered as the wind began to blow.

"Infernal night, we command thee," we said.

The small flames exploded into a blinding light and wrapped around our circle as the wind howled.

"Eden, you need to move into the middle now," my mother urged.

I stared at the empty spot in the middle of the circle. My palms began to sweat and they released my hands.

I took a hesitant step toward the center.

"Hurry, Eden," Rafael said. "Like a good soufflé, timing is critical."

I pushed aside any misgivings and leaped into the middle. I pulled the charmed bottle from my pocket.

The pressure continued to build as the demon fought against the spell.

I concentrated on absorbing the energy around me. I

pulled it toward me, the magic so powerful that I worried my body would explode like a supernova.

"Open the bottle now," Neville yelled.

I popped off the cork and the open mouth seemed to suck all the fog around us. Gray clouds rushed past me and I cemented my feet in the ground so as not to lose my balance. It felt like herds of dinosaurs were trampling me, but I held my ground. If only Agent Redmond could see me now, he'd think twice about forcing me to complete my so-called training.

Once the air was completely clear, I popped the cork back in, sealing the demon inside the warded bottle.

"The stars," my mother said, glancing skyward. "I can see them shining again."

My family wandered away to admire the glittering sky over the bay, leaving Neville and me to clean up the mess. He collected the rune rocks and placed them at the bottom of the backpack.

I stooped to pick up the bowl and stared at the contents. "I used my blood, Neville."

He came to stand beside me. "It was the best way to defeat the demon, Eden."

"So what? If you can't beat 'em, join 'em? That's not really how it's supposed to work."

Neville gently removed the bowl from my hands. "There's no 'supposed to.' Your job is to protect this town from supernatural interference, and you did."

"But at what cost?" I asked.

"You did a good thing tonight, Eden," he said. "Lives were at stake. For Hecate's sake, lives were lost. Imagine the catastrophes that could have taken place if you hadn't put an end to the impulses."

The impulses.

My stomach knotted as my thoughts turned to Chief Fox.

"I kissed the chief."

Neville halted. "You kissed him?"

I nodded. "On the lips." I picked up the remaining herbs that hadn't disintegrated.

"Thank you for the anatomical clarification," he said. "You realize it was only the result of the demon's influence, though."

Neville was right and yet...

"I like him," I said.

"I like him, too. He's proving to be an excellent choice for chief of police."

I heaved a sigh. "No, Neville. I'm not talking about on a professional level, though I do agree with you."

"You mean you'd like to date him?"

"Yes. No. Maybe." My heart pounded at the very idea of dating him. "That kiss wasn't for the sake of kissing someone, Neville. It was because I wanted to kiss *him,* specifically." It was an impulse I'd been fighting from the moment I met him in The Cheese Wheel and drunkenly mistook him for a stripper.

"I see." Neville conjured a spell to dispose of the toxic materials in the bowl. Then he wrapped the bowl in a cloth and placed it in the backpack.

"What does that mean?" I asked, following closely behind him.

"It means I understand the words you're saying to me."

"But you don't approve."

Neville frowned. "You don't report to me, Eden. I report to you. My approval is neither here nor there."

"I can't like him. He's the chief of police." And human. And completely ignorant of our existence.

"You can like him," Neville said. "Liking him—that simply involves feelings. I'm just not certain that it's wise to act on them."

185

"You sound like my mother."

We put the last of the items into the backpack and Neville zipped it. "You already know it's a violation of FBM rules. It also could be dangerous. For you. For him." His eyes were downcast. "I don't know how to advise you on a matter of the heart."

"You've never been in a situation like this?"

"I've never been in love," Neville said simply.

"Whoa, I didn't say anything about love," I said. "I haven't even been able to properly explore like."

Neville gave me a small smile. "And you worry about becoming evil?"

I stopped short. "What does any of this have to do with becoming evil?"

He shook his head. "Think about it. You're concerned for him because you care for him. You're concerned with breaking the rules because you care about the FBM and your reputation. You *care*, Agent Fury. Evildoers don't care. They do what they want when they want and damn the consequences."

"What about the fact that I'm willing to consider breaking the rules for my own selfish purposes?" I asked. "That seems like a slippery slope to Evil Town."

Neville slung the backpack over his shoulder. "If I notice any questionable actions on your part, I promise to bring them to your attention."

I bumped his hip. "You'd do that for me?"

"I'm your assistant. It's my job." He paused. "But I'd also do it as your friend."

My heart warmed. "Thanks, Neville. It's nice to know you're on my side." Other than Clara, I'd never had anyone truly on my side—not anyone who knew the truth about me.

"You're a good egg, Agent Fury," he said. "Maybe one of these days you'll start to believe it yourself."

CHAPTER NINETEEN

WHEN I AWOKE the next morning, I knew something was different. I just didn't know what. I fled the attic and ran to the bathroom mirror to inspect myself.

"Damn, where did that zit come from?" I pushed my face closer to the glass to examine the angry bump on my chin. "How do I get to be twenty-six and still have pimple problems?" Normally I would suspect a hex, but I couldn't think of a reason for it. Not that my family needed a reason. They performed hexes for sport.

A knock on the bathroom door startled me. "Hurry up in there. I'm an old lady. If you take too long, you might be stepping over my corpse."

I opened the door for Grandma. "You say that like it's a bad thing."

"Aren't you a sassy one now that you've defeated a demon?" She brushed past me. "I can tell you're not done in here, but an elderly woman's bladder awaits no man...or fury."

"I was checking for a new power," I admitted. "I feel different, but I don't see any sign of it."

187

Grandma looked me up and down. "I'll tell you what I told your mother when she got her first period." She paused dramatically. "I'm sorry."

"Thank you for your condolences." I left the bathroom before she could hike up her nightgown in front of me. It wouldn't surprise me to learn Grandma was part of the public urination problem during the chaos demon's reign.

I made my way to the kitchen where Anton and Olivia were building a house of cards.

"Do I look different to you?" I asked.

Anton studied me. "You have that zit on your chin. Is that it?" He stopped. "No, wait. You always seem to have blemishes."

I folded my arms. "Gee, thanks for the ego boost."

Anton grinned. "What are big brothers for?"

Olivia climbed down from the chair and came closer to inspect me. "You have flames in your eyes."

I frowned at her. "Excuse me?"

She pointed to my face. "Your eyes. I see flames."

I pulled out my phone and used the mirror app to check my reflection. Sure enough, I saw orange flames dancing in the pupils. I yanked down my phone and stared at my brother.

"What does that mean?"

"Relax," Anton said. "It's not like humans can see a thing like that. And it'll probably be a turn-on for a demon."

Olivia glanced at her dad. "What's a turn-on?"

"Like a light switch," he said quickly. "You flip it on."

"Something that makes one individual attractive to another," I said, shaking my head at my brother.

"I think you're pretty, Aunt Eden," Olivia said. "But I don't care if your eyes have fire."

"Whose eyes have fire?" My mother appeared on the other side of the kitchen.

"Mine," I said. "Tiny orange flames. I think it's a new fury power."

"Doesn't sound like much of a power," Anton scoffed. "What're you going to do—use them to roast marshmallows?"

"I don't know that actual fire shoots out of my eyes," I said.

"Try it," Olivia said, with a little too much enthusiasm. She was going to be a full-on demon for sure. I worried that none of her mother's druid DNA made it into that compact body.

"I'm not Superman," I objected. "I don't have laser vision."

"So now you can fly *and* have laser vision," Anton said. "If you can jump tall buildings in a single bound, then you're totally Superman."

I groaned. "I don't..." There was no point in arguing. I'd just have to see whether I could, in fact, shoot flames from my eyeballs like some kind of misfit dragon.

"Here." My mother handed me a plant. "I never liked this one. See if you can disintegrate it."

I held the plant and focused on the stems. I narrowed my eyes and tried to force my energy toward it.

Nothing happened.

"I don't think I have eyeballs of fire," I said.

"Well, that's disappointing," Olivia said.

Grandma emerged from the hallway still in her robe and slippers. "Why are you staring at my Christmas cactus?"

I quickly handed the plant to my mother. "I was admiring it."

"Aunt Eden has flames in her eyes," Olivia said.

"Snitch," I hissed.

Grandma focused on me. "Flames in your eyes? Is that what you were looking for in the bathroom?"

"I didn't notice them," I said. "I was looking for something more dramatic."

"Flames in your eyes is pretty dramatic," Grandma said. She bustled over to the stovetop to put on the kettle. "Do you know what it means?"

"Means?" I asked. Anton and I exchanged quizzical looks. "So they don't *do* anything?"

"No, they're symbolic. The eternal flame," Grandma said. She filled the kettle with water and turned on the stove. "Means you're immortal now. Congratulations."

My mouth dropped open.

"What's immortal?" Olivia asked.

"It means your aunt is like a vampire," Anton said slowly. "She will live forever."

"Nothing can kill you?" Olivia asked, looking up at me with wide eyes.

"No, that's invincibility," I said. "You can be killed as an immortal, but it's harder."

"And if nothing kills you, then you live forever," my mother added. Her gaze was fixated on me. "You'll outlive us all, Eden."

"Can I do that?" Olivia asked. She turned her eager face to her father. "I want to be immortal, too."

"You're not a fury," Anton said.

Olivia stomped her foot. "Why not? Why do I have to be a stupid demon?"

"Why do I have to be a stupid fury?" I asked quietly.

"Are you sure that's what the flames mean?" my mother asked Grandma.

The kettle whistled and Grandma removed it from the heat. "I'm sure."

"I'll look it up," my mother said. She pulled out her phone.

"You don't believe me?" Grandma glared at my mother. "I'm old, therefore, my knowledge is shaky?"

"I didn't say that," my mother said, as she clicked on her phone. "Siri, do flames in a supernatural's eyes represent the eternal flame?"

Siri's robotic yet soothing voice piped up. "Flames in certain supernatural's eyes are a reflection of that supernatural's immortality."

My mother gaped at me. "She's right."

"Who's 'she'—the cat's pajamas?" Grandma asked. "I'm your mother. Show me some respect."

"That's amazing, Eden," my mother said. "You're so lucky."

Lucky? I didn't feel lucky. I felt horrible. The more fury I became, the less normal I was. How could I lead as normal and good a life as possible when I knew I'd live forever? My mind drifted to the image of Henry staked on the fencepost. Would that be my fate?

I felt a small hand slip into mine and realized Olivia had come over to comfort me.

"Don't be sad, Aunt Eden," she said. "I'm glad you'll always be around."

The doorbell rang, which sent Princess Buttercup and Charlemagne charging toward the front door. Candy remained sprawled across the windowsill, unconcerned.

"Eden, it's Agent Redmond," Aunt Thora called from the foyer.

"I was hoping for at least a day to recuperate before I take the final training tests," I said. I squeezed Olivia's hand once before releasing it and went to the door. Agent Redmond stood framed in the doorway in his suit and dark sunglasses.

"Hey, my future's so bright, you have to wear shades," I said.

"Thanks to you I get to wear them again," he said. He flipped them to the top of his head. "Why don't you come outside where we can talk?"

I stepped onto the front porch and closed the door behind me. "You're not going to conduct the tests right here, are you? My family won't hesitate to mock me."

"I'm not going to conduct the tests at all," he said.

I balked. "I'm sorry. Come again?"

"You've demonstrated more than adequate skills to hold this position, Agent Fury," Agent Redmond said. "As far as I'm concerned, you've passed with flying colors. We're having the time of our lives."

"That's against regulations, Agent," I said, wagging a finger. "The demon's influence on you should be gone by now."

He gave me a sympathetic look. "I'm willing to make allowances, under the circumstances. You expended a lot of powerful energy to defeat that demon."

I rolled up my sleeves. "I need to prove I can do this."

"You want to prove yourself to me after all my haranguing," Agent Redmond said. "I get it."

"No, I want to prove myself to...myself." I rubbed my hands together. "Where do we start?" I started to walk down the porch steps but he moved to block me.

"It isn't necessary, Agent Fury."

"Nobody puts Eden in a corner," I said.

He chuckled. "You've done the lift, Agent Fury. The moment you stepped inside that circle."

"Neville told you about it?"

He nodded. "He's very impressed by you."

"He'll be even more impressed now. I received a gift from the gods today."

His brow lifted. "A new fury power?"

"Yep."

"I can't say I'm surprised," he said. "It sounds like you absorbed a lot of magic." He placed a hand on my shoulder. "But you saved the town. Bright side, right?"

"Yes, but at what personal cost?" One more fury power. One stop closer to Badville aboard the Evil Express.

"Some moments are greater than ourselves," Agent Redmond said. "You have a connection to this place that others don't. You understand the nuances of Chipping Cheddar better than any agent coming in cold. Even Paul Pidcock fell short in that regard and he lived here a long time."

I raised a skeptical eyebrow. "Chipping Cheddar has nuances?"

Agent Redmond leaned against the siding. "Agent Fury, you're underestimating this town and your attachment to it. It's in your skin. It's part of you. One of the reasons you were able to defeat the demon is because you have insight into this place and its people."

"I have a ghost informant," I said. "Don't give me too much credit."

Agent Redmond smiled, softening his angular features. "Why not? You don't give yourself enough."

A thought occurred to me. "Agent Redmond, a quick question about the personality test."

"What about it?"

"When two people have the same personality type," I began, "how does that play out in real life?"

His brow furrowed. "I'm not sure what you're asking, Agent Fury."

I couldn't say too much without throwing Grandma under the bus, not that I was necessarily opposed to that idea in a literal sense.

"My grandmother and I—we're both ENTJ's, but we're nothing alike."

He winked. "Apparently not."

My stomach sank. Forget my fury powers, even my personality was leading me down a dark path.

193

"If it's any consolation," he said, "I'm a Slytherin, according to Pottermore."

My eyes bulged. "You? No way."

He shrugged. "I know, right? I always considered myself more of a Hufflepuff."

I would've said Ravenclaw, personally, but I kept that thought to myself.

"It's not the worst thing in the world, you know, to be like your grandmother."

I started to choke. "You met her. How can you say that?"

"Your family helped to stop the demon. They didn't have to do that."

They helped stop the demon because it was in their self-interest, not because it was the right thing to do. My family was perfectly willing to pitch in when it suited them. That fact didn't make them less evil—it just made them, in this case, the lesser of two.

"What about Princess Buttercup?" I asked.

Agent Redmond's expression remained blank.

"Are you going to make me apply for a license to keep her?" I continued. "You know they'll take her away."

The agent's nostrils flared. "I don't know what you're talking about, Agent Fury. What hellhound?"

The knot in my stomach loosened. "Thank you."

"For what, Agent Fury? You're the one who did all the work."

And, finally, the question I dreaded to ask. "What about Clara?" She was my best friend and I knew she didn't allow herself the luxury of developing feelings for someone very often.

"We've said our goodbyes. She's been an unexpected breath of fresh air." He heaved a regretful sigh. "I'll miss her."

"Not enough to stay?" I asked. "You could take my job and date Clara. A win-win."

"We all have our callings. I'm afraid mine is training. Besides, this town is in safe hands with you, Agent Fury. I'm not sure I'd be up to the task."

"Come back and see us again," I said. "I guess the FBM will want to know how Neville and I are doing."

"There are progress checks," he said. "If it's at all feasible, then I'll make sure I'm assigned to conduct yours."

"Safe travels, Agent Redmond."

"Welcome to the team, Agent Fury." He shook my hand before returning to his rental car.

As I walked back into the house, I sent Clara a text to make sure she was okay. I had to imagine his departure would be difficult for her.

"Such a delightful man." My mother stood at the island in the kitchen, chopping peppers. "You should've snagged him for yourself instead of letting Clara have him."

"I didn't *let* Clara have him. They genuinely liked each other. Anyway, he's not sticking around, so it doesn't matter." I grabbed a banana from the bowl and fled to the attic before anyone else could say a word.

Alice was on the mattress watching *Dirty Dancing*.

"Again?" I asked.

"One more time before I move on to *The Princess Bride*," she said.

"That's a classic. You'll love it." I propped my pillow behind me and leaned against the wall.

"You've had quite a time of it recently," Alice said.

I nodded. "I think I could sleep for a week if my family would let me."

Alice put an apparitional arm around me. "I know you can't feel it, but I'm offering you a comforting squeeze."

I smiled. "Thanks."

"What's wrong, dear? You've saved the town from a

demon and passed your training test. You should be elated right now."

"Elated isn't the word I'd use." Not when the price was so high.

"Is it your new fury power?"

"That…and Chief Fox," I said.

"Ah. Your beau."

"He's not my beau. It was just the demon's influence that made us kiss."

"That demon's specialty was impulse control. It didn't make you want things you don't actually want or feel things you don't actually feel," Alice said.

I looked at her. "Stop making sense. It hurts my head."

"I think you're underestimating Chief Fox, just like you underestimate yourself."

"I appreciate the advice, Alice, but it's over."

"Why does it have to be over?" Alice asked. "Why not use what happened as an opportunity to move your relationship forward? He can court you."

"He can't court me, Alice," I said. "Mostly because courting isn't a thing in this century."

"That's too bad," Alice said. "Courting is a wonderful time to get to know each other."

"The chief can't know me any better than he does now."

The ghost regarded me with a critical eye. "Can't or you won't let him?"

I opened my mouth to respond but then quickly closed it again. I didn't know how to explain to her that I was still too uncomfortable in my own skin to ever make anyone else feel comfortable with me.

"I have an important job to focus on," I said.

"There are more important things in life than chasing demons," Alice said.

"Tell that to Manfred's wife or Lizette, or the other people whose lives have been irrevocably changed by supernatural interferences."

The sound of Princess Buttercup's bark reached my ears.

"Is there a problem?" Alice asked.

"No, that's her happy bark," I said. I went to the window and peered outside. "Oh."

Chief Fox was on the front lawn, petting Princess Buttercup's head. The hellhound was surprisingly fond of the human.

I opened the window and poked my head outside. "Hi, Chief."

He shaded his eyes from the sun and looked up at me. "Do you have a minute?"

"Hold on a sec," I replied and ducked back inside. I felt ready to throw up.

"Go on," Alice urged. "See what he does now that the demon's influence is gone."

"That's exactly why I *don't* want to go down." I was torn between hoping the heat between us was real and hoping it was due to a mutual lack of impulse control. It was easier to keep up my guard around him when I believed the feelings were one-sided. The possibility that he might feel the same...

I flew downstairs and out the front door at fury speed before any family members could intercept him.

"That was fast," he commented.

"I needed the exercise."

"If you feel like walking, how about showing me the progress on that barn of yours? I'd love to see it."

"Okay."

Princess Buttercup ran ahead and I walked with the chief around the house to the backyard.

"I wanted to let you know that the historical society received enough donations to raise the remains of the Brizo from the bay."

"That's wonderful news," I said. Once the ship was raised, I'd be able to put the souls to rest.

"Most of the money came from descendants of the…" He scratched his head. "I hate to call them murderers."

"It was a complicated time, but they were ultimately responsible for the deaths of everyone on that ship."

The chief looked at me. "You tend to see things as black and white, don't you?"

"You're law enforcement. Don't you?"

"I used to," he said. "But I'll be honest—the older I get, the more I'm willing to see shades of gray."

"Well, you saw a lot of shades of gray this week with the fog," I joked.

We arrived at the barn and I opened the door to show him inside.

"This looks fantastic," Chief Fox said. His gaze traveled over the wooden flooring and the solid beams above. "John's doing tremendous work."

"He is," I agreed. "I can't wait until it's finished."

The chief moved to close the barn door behind us. "I also wanted to talk about what happened at The Cheese Wheel."

My stomach plummeted. The expression on his face suggested that the talk was going to be more of an apology.

I held up a hand. "You don't have to say anything, Chief. It was in the heat of the moment. I know it didn't mean anything."

He frowned. "But it did mean something, at least to me."

"Oh."

We stood in the center of the empty barn, staring at each other.

"In truth, I've been wanting to kiss you since the moment I met you that night at The Cheese Wheel."

"Really?" I squeaked.

"I wasn't sure if you just had a thing for strippers in cop uniforms." A smile tugged at the sides of his mouth.

"I've never actually seen a real stripper," I said, "so I don't know." *That* was my response? Kill me now.

The chief didn't seem deterred by my admission. "How would you feel about going on a date with me? Maybe put the dinner part before the amazing kissing."

How would I feel? Amazing. Ebullient. Hopeful. Terrified.

"I don't know if that's a good idea," I said. In fact, I *knew* it wasn't a good idea. Rule number one told me so.

"Because of our jobs?" he asked.

"Yes." Although I couldn't elaborate.

"If you're not interested, it's okay," he said. "Feel free to tell me to go on my merry way."

"Your merry way?" I repeated. "You're an elf now?"

He inched closer to me. "Sometimes I think we're on the same page and then other times..." He trailed off.

"It's complicated," I said.

"Not to me. You either want to pursue this or you don't."

I gazed at him longingly. As much as I wanted to pursue this...

"Kiss him!" Alice's shrill voice penetrated my head.

"I can't," I said.

"It can't be that agent friend of yours, right?" Chief Fox asked. "The one who looks like Legolas, except for the hair? I saw him with Clara."

"No, he left," I said. "And we're not involved."

To his credit, the chief didn't push the issue. "However complicated it is, I'm sure we can work through it if we want it badly enough."

Oh, I wanted it badly enough. He just had no idea how complicated the complications really were. And now I was immortal on top of everything else.

I struggled to choose the right words. "I look forward to

kissing you again sometime in the future, when life is less challenging."

"That's false hope," Alice said, hovering by the arched window. "You just gave the chief of police false hope. It's practically a crime."

His mouth twitched. "Sometime in the future is pretty vague, but I'll take it." He opened the barn door and beams of sunlight came streaming in. His gaze swept the interior of the barn one last time. "I think you're going to be very happy here."

My chest tightened. "I hope so."

I watched with mixed emotions as he left the barn and vanished in a blaze of light.

* * *

Keep an eye out for **Grace Under Fury**, Book 4 in the Federal Bureau of Magic cozy mystery series.

ALSO BY ANNABEL CHASE

Thank you for reading *No Guts, No Fury*. Sign up for my newsletter and receive a FREE Starry Hollow Witches short story— http://eepurl.com/ctYNzf. You can also like me on Facebook so you can find out about the next book before it's even available.

Other books by Annabel Chase include:

Starry Hollow Witches

Magic & Murder, Book 1

Magic & Mystery, Book 2

Magic & Mischief, Book 3

Magic & Mayhem, Book 4

Magic & Mercy, Book 5

Magic & Madness, Book 6

Magic & Malice, Book 7

Magic & Mythos, Book 8

Outlier, Sentry of the South, Book 1

Outfox, Sentry of the South, Book 2

Outbreak, Sentry of the South, Book 3

Outwit, Enforcer of the East, Book 1

Outlaw, Enforcer of the East, Book 2

Outrun, Keeper of the North, Book 1

Outgrow, Keeper of the North, Book 2